STAY WITH ME

ERIN TREJO

STAY WITH ME

ERIN TREJO

1

CALLAN

Everything is a clusterfuck right now. No one was who we expected them to be. To learn that the people you trusted were really your enemies really tore me apart. I tried to put up a good front for my brothers but in reality, it's hit me pretty hard.

I always knew the plan to kill our dad was inevitable. He was ruining us, ruining our family. He was tearing me and my brothers apart. I don't think that's what's really bothering me though. There's something more and I can feel the secrets of the past as they linger in the air.

We've since moved back into my dad's house. It's far bigger than ours was and the fact that there is so much paperwork and books to go through, it just made sense. Now I'm not so sure. The evil, the darkness that surrounded him seems to be creeping into me while inside these walls. I don't think Steele or Knox feel it the way I do. I don't know what it is or what's happening, but I have a bad feeling things are going to go from bad to worse before we know it.

"What the hell is your problem?" Steele asks as I drop onto the couch and lean back. I don't feel like dealing with his shit today.

"Nothing."

"You've been a dick since we moved back here. Is that what it is? You don't want to be here?" I roll my eyes and sit up, resting my elbows on my knees.

"I'm not a baby, Steele. If I want to leave, I damn well will."

"By all means little brother, get the fuck to it then. No one wants to deal with you stomping around like a little bitch," Knox chimes in. I flip them both off before pulling my joint out and lighting it up. Inhaling deeply, I let that sweet sticky goodness coat my lungs and take away the edge that I'm feeling.

"Seriously, what is it, Cal?" Steele asks watching me.

"I don't know, Steele. I feel like there's something inside of me that's coming unhinged."

"You're turning into us," Steele says casually as if it's not a big deal. To them, they've always had this arrogant bully type quality but I've never had that. I've always been the calmer, nicer of the three of us and yet there is something nagging me now.

"God fucking help me," I grumble and bring the joint back to my lips.

"We need to talk anyway," Knox adds.

"About what?"

"Now that Dad is gone, college isn't a necessity. I for one am not continuing," Steele says. That isn't a shock to me. I didn't figure he would, although running this family, running all the companies has never been his thing. He never wanted a part of it and I totally understood, but now? I don't know.

"I'm sticking it out. I've already started, and I might as well finish my degree." They both look to me with raised eyebrows.

"Plan on leaving Rolling Springs?" Knox asks the question that is sitting on the tip of both of their tongues.

"No. I don't want to give up football just yet, either."

"Or seeing Shane every day." Steele chuckles.

"I'm still unsure of all that," I add. Both of their heads snap back to look at me. They didn't expect that answer.

"What? You know that was all Dad, right?" Steele, the voice of reason when it comes to anything related to our dad, states.

"Was it though? She seemed to slink off pretty easily," I remind him.

"You dumped her, man. You treated her like shit. What did you expect her to do?" This is from Knox.

"I don't know. Question me? Ask why I did it? I don't fucking know."

"Girls don't want to question that shit," Whisper says as she strolls into the room with a bottle of whiskey in her hand. I watch her bring it to her lips, taking a long pull.

"Why the hell not?" I ask looking up at her. She walks over and sits, making herself comfortable in my lap as Steele growls from across the room.

"You left us. Why would we want a reason for it? All we know is that you did it and now we hate you for it," she says slurring her words. It's been nice having Whisper around all the time. It's not that I like her in that way but she's an all-out great person. Not that she isn't sexy as hell and gorgeous she just isn't my style.

"You might want to get off his lap now," Steele growls once more. Whisper rolls her eyes and adjusts herself in my lap. My cock thickens in my jeans. I'm still a man even if she is my brother's.

"Nah, Callan likes me right here." Whisper takes another drink, Knox laughs.

"I'm serious. You wouldn't even wonder why a guy broke up with you?" I ask her. She shakes her head.

"I've never had a boyfriend, Callan. I wouldn't know but I do know that every single time I was moved from one place to another, I wondered. I wondered why they didn't want me but once I got older, I realized it really didn't matter anymore. People come and go in your life. You can't spend that time asking questions. You're wasting time." Wrapping my arms around her waist I pull her back against my chest and relax into the couch. Whisper curls up in my arms and rests her head on my chest.

"Thanks, Whisper."

"For what?" she asks, looking up at me.

"Being you. Being here." She smiles and nods slightly when Steele's chair hits the wall. Whisper and I laugh right before she's being jerked off my lap. He doesn't give her time to speak, just tosses her over his shoulder, spanks her ass, and carries her out of the office.

"You never answered," I say to Knox.

"What? About school?" I nod. "I honestly haven't thought much about it, Cal. Everything has happened so quickly. I hate school but I kind of agree with you. The degree could come into play later on especially with all the damn companies." Hearing him admit that makes me grin. Knox isn't as stupid as he likes to pretend to be.

"It's a good move. I mean fuck, we're all only a year apart but Steele is taking lead for now and I think once he gets tired of it, we're going to have to step up. I know this isn't what either of you wanted," I tell him.

"It's not but it's also life. This is our lives now. The businesses, the family. All of it. I think we all need to work together on this shit whether we like it or not." I nod because I totally agree with him. We have to step up and be the men we were meant to be.

"I'm going to the studio," I tell him as I shove off the couch and stand, stretching my arms above my head.

"It looks like you need to hit the gym." He laughs nodding toward my abs. I flip him off causing him to laugh harder.

"Don't you want to go stalk Leddy?" I ask as I head for the door.

"Not right now. I'm taking a nap!" I watch my brother as he sprawls out on the couch across the room, closing his eyes.

Maybe being in this house isn't going to be as bad as I think it is.

2
————

SHANE

I answer the phones and sit at a desk. This has become my weekends and after-school gig. Alder Dance Company. Who the hell would have thought I'd end up working for them? I surely didn't. Now, this is the only place I go aside from school.

"You're here early," Leddy says as she strolls in the front doors. I look up and smile at her as she drops her bag on the floor and looks over her shoulder.

"You okay?" Quickly her head snaps back in my direction, her smile back in place.

"Yeah, I'm good. Any of the guys here yet?" she asks. I shake my head.

"Not yet. Just me," I tell her. She nods and bends down to grab her bag when Callan walks in. He moves quickly, rushing in behind her and grabbing her hips in his hands. Pressing his cock against her ass, she laughs and stands up quickly.

"You Alder men are such horn balls." She laughs as she looks over her shoulder at him.

"We can't help it when we see a nice ass in a pair of leggings. Maybe you should rethink your wardrobe." His eyes sparkle with mischief until he looks over at me, then it all disappears.

"Or maybe you should use your hand a little more in the shower." Callan nods but his eyes stay on mine. They almost seem darker than normal.

"I'll see you in class," he says quickly before walking away.

"What the hell was that about?" Leddy turns back to me.

"I have no idea. He's been like this since they moved back into their dad's house. He's distant."

"Don't let him push you away, Shane. You know how these guys are," she says pointing at me.

"I know. I just didn't think we would be back to this," I admit.

"He's dealing with some stuff. All that shit with his dad and Whisper, it has to weigh pretty heavy on him too, you know?" She's probably right. Although he was fine for the few days we were out of Rolling Springs, as soon as we were back everything changed. I thought we were closer, talking more but now he's just as distant as he's ever been. It stings a little to know the one person that you crave to have on your side isn't there anymore.

"I know."

"See you after class. We'll get lunch," Leddy says before turning and heading down the hallway. I drop back into my chair and look at the computer screen in front of me blankly. I don't know what's gotten into Callan or why he's pushing me away but maybe Leddy's right. Maybe I need to push back. The phone rings and when I glance down I realize that it's coming from one of the rooms and I grab it quickly.

"Yes?"

"We need some towels down here," Callan says quickly before the line goes dead. Rolling my eyes, I shove out of my chair and grab the towels from the closet, carrying them down the hall. When I step into the room Callan's in, he surprises me. He slams the door shut behind me and in seconds, the towels hit the floor and I'm pressed against the wall. My heart beats out of my chest as he breathes against my neck.

"Where'd the bruise come from?"

"What are you talking about?"

"You think I don't know when you wear extra makeup, Shane?" he hisses, his warm breath fanning against my flesh.

"Maybe I just felt like wearing extra today," I tell him while trying to keep my breathing even. It's a chore when he's this close to me.

"You're lying and you know how much I hate that."

"You're different," I say, clearing my throat. Callan pulls back and looks me in the eye, his gaze full of confusion.

"What do you mean?"

"You're different. What's going on with you?" I risk the chance and ask. I need to know. I can't do this hot and cold thing he has going on.

"There's nothing going on with me. I'm the same as I've always been." He takes a step back and my stomach drops.

"No, you're different."

"Then maybe I'm becoming who I was meant to be, Shane! What difference does it make?"

"You don't want me anymore do you?" Taking the chance and asking is hard for me but the fact is, I need to know. If he is going to be like this, I'm not so sure that I want to be with him.

"Oh, I do want you," he says stepping back into my space.

"You don't act like it."

"I want you to the point it makes me sick. I want you and I hate it. Don't you get that part?" His jaw is locked in place and nothing he's saying makes any sense. I start to step around him to leave when his hand grips my hip roughly. So roughly that I wince. "Don't walk away from me."

"You do it to me all the time." Shoving his hand away, I move around him and head out of the room as quickly as possible. Flying down the hallway, I'm back at the desk when Whisper walks in. She eyes me for a long second before leaning over the counter. She flicks my hair over my shoulder, brushes her fingers down my cheek and sighs.

"Why do you look so sad?"

"Callan's being a dick." She laughs at my choice of words.

"He's been different lately. I don't know what his problem is," she adds, seeing the look on my face. I know Whisper knows something is going on, but no one knows what.

"Yeah, that's an understatement."

"Did you talk to him?" she asks.

"Does him pinning me in the room count as talking? Or the fact that he said he wants me and that makes him sick?"

"He said that?" she squeals, her eyebrows shooting up.

"His exact words."

"That asshole! I'll deal with his ass!" she says standing up straight and grabbing her bag. I nearly laugh when I see the look on her face. She's pissed.

"Don't you dare. It'll make it worse. I'll deal with him later."

"You sure? I don't mind kicking his balls into his throat," she says in a serious tone. In fact, I know she would. This is why I like Whisper. She takes no shit from anyone.

"Maybe next time." She smiles and shakes her head before walking down the hall. When she stops, she looks over her shoulder at me and says, "Go a shade darker next time." I automatically know that she's talking about my makeup job. Nodding, I sit back in my chair and sigh. This is going to be a long day.

3

CALLAN

"Who the hell invited her?" I ask Knox as he unloads the coolers out of the back of the truck.

"Whisper," he says. Should have known. Those two are best fucking friends anymore. I didn't want Shane here. Although the bonfire is for anyone that wants to come, I was hoping she wouldn't. There're things that I've learned about her over the past week and I don't like it. Something doesn't settle in me the way I thought it would.

When Shane first moved to Rolling Springs, she was a lost little girl. Hell, she still is, but we had no reason to suspect she was anything other than what we saw so we didn't do much digging into her life or family. They seemed quiet enough and kept to themselves and that served them well in our town. Now? Now I feel like I missed something with her, and I went in search to find it out. Her truth? Her truth is public record although I won't share a word of it with my brothers, not unless she forces my hand. I know her secret and it rips my heart out of my chest too. When I saw the words printed on paper, I almost lost it. Now she will be on the receiving end of my rage and anger. She needs to know what it all feels like. What she did.

I shake my head and try to calm my nerves when Steele slaps a hand on my shoulder.

"You okay?"

"Fine." Brushing him off, I grab a beer from the cooler and walk toward the fire that's barely burning. Grabbing the gas, I pour some on and watch as the flames lick the night sky. I've missed these bonfires. Dad didn't like them much. He didn't like that we'd invite half the town to join in either. He thought the elites; the founding families needed to stick together and keep everyone else out. That's not how we felt though. We wanted more out of life. We wanted to mingle and see the people. That's why Steele decided to do this.

"Hey," a voice says next to me. I turn and look over at a girl I've seen around school before. I don't know her name because she isn't one of us.

"Hey yourself," I smile.

"I'm Gina. Thanks for inviting everyone. It's weird going to school with you guys and not really knowing who you are," she says as I raise an eyebrow. This is true too. We don't mingle well, or at least we haven't in the past. Gina is pretty. Brown hair that she has tied up on top of her head. She isn't bad looking if I'm being honest.

"Callan," I say extending my hand. She takes it in hers, a blush spreading across her face.

"Everyone knows who you are." She smirks.

"Suppose that's true but I don't know you. Why don't you come sit with me?" Out of the corner of my eye, I can see Shane. She's watching me intently through the flames that flicker in the sky. Gina nods and walks with me over to a set of chairs. I motion for her to take a seat and then pass her a beer.

"You've been here for a few years, right?" I ask watching her nod as she takes a long pull from her bottle.

"Yeah. I went to the high school here but that was just senior year. I can't wait to get out of here," she says looking up at me with big brown eyes.

"Why? Are we that bad?" The anger inside of me seems to be bubbling out of control. It's building and building and I'm afraid when it erupts nothing will be the same.

"No, I didn't say that. It's just this is a small town and all. I want more out of life," she says bringing her bottle back to her lips. This one's a drinker.

"What do you want to do?"

"I want to be a photographer. I want to go around the world taking pictures of everything, capture their beauty."

"Sounds boring." She looks up at me and I shrug. I guess after the life that I've lived, you don't see the beauty in things like that.

"Then I'd say you have a sad outlook on life. Don't you want to see the world outside of Rolling Springs?" she asks. That stab of fury in my chest ignites. I shove out of my chair and eye her for a long second before walking away. I toss my bottle in the fire and head toward the truck for something stronger. Opening the back door, I dig around until I find the Jack and pull it out.

"What are you doing?"

"Drinking."

"Did you hit her?" Leave it to Whisper to be so damn blunt. I unscrew the cap and take a long pull before looking over at her and shaking my head.

"I don't hit women. Thought you knew that," I hiss in her direction as she shrugs her shoulders.

"I don't know as much as I thought I did about you, Callan. You're turning into them."

"Into who?"

"Your brothers."

"So? What's wrong with being like them? You don't seem to mind fucking my brother the way he is." That might have been a low blow, but it needed to be said. A slow smile pulls across her face as she steps closer to me.

"I never said there was anything wrong with being like them, Callan. It's nice to finally see you come out of your little protective shell that your dad kept you locked in." Her words fire me up more than I thought they would. Grabbing her around the throat, I slam her against the truck as visions of seeing her in his clothes flash behind my eyes.

"Stop pushing me, Whisper."

"Why? Look at you," she says. I drag my gaze to meet hers and the smile I see does something to my insides. Is she right? Have I been holding back because of my dad?

"What's this?" I hear Steele's voice before he leans against the truck next to his girl.

"This is Callan becoming himself."

"You might want to take your hands off my girl before shit gets heated, brother." Steele's voice is hard, and I know he isn't playing but there's a part of me that wants to push my luck with him. Maybe that's what I need. A good fight.

"I kind of like my hands on her. You remember the pool house, Whisper?" Her eyes shoot to mine and there's heat in them that I didn't expect. Steele grumbles something under his breath but it's Whisper that pushes her body closer to mine. I slowly ease the grip I have on her throat before she wraps her arms around my waist.

"Even if I wanted to, I'm not a cheater, Cal. I love you too much to take that part away from you." Her words are like a slap to the face although I understand what she's saying. I wouldn't really touch her again since she's with Steele now. I just can't figure out what the hell has gotten into me lately. Leaning down, I press my lips to the top of her head and sigh.

"I know. I love you too, Whisper."

4

SHANE

"I'm glad you stuck around," I tell Whisper as we walk toward the football field.

"Me too. I hate school but I want to be able to have a degree while working in the studio. I just need something to fall back on, you know," she says as she braids her long black hair over her shoulder.

"I would hate to be here by myself," I mumble.

"By yourself? You have Callan. He's just being a prick lately. Like his brothers," she chimes in with a laugh.

"He's so different. He's changed."

"Change is good though, right?" She looks to me. I just shrug. I don't know if it is or not anymore. Whisper and I stroll into the locker room and all eyes turn our way. Some of the guy's smile, others look away but it's his that burn a hole through me. Callan watches me like I'm about to steal something. The way his gaze moves over my body causes my nerves to fire off.

"Hey, Knox! Come give us an interview," Whisper yells.

Knox smirks but stands and walks over to us. The other guys are talking and getting ready for their showers when Callan moves. He grabs the paper out of my hand shoving it roughly into Whisper's before gripping my wrist. He pulls me roughly toward the back before shoving me against the shower wall.

"What are you doing?" I ask as he reaches around and starts the shower. I'm fully clothed but he doesn't seem to mind. The water turns on and sprays around me before he jerks me under it.

"What the hell, Callan?"

"You looked a little hot, Shane. Staring at all the guys out there." His voice is low and husky.

"Are you insane? I wasn't starring at anyone! Let me go!" I try to move away from him, but he keeps me held under the spray. My clothes are sticking to my skin, the heat in the room is consuming me.

"You want something, Shane?" His eyes are full of hunger, but I can also see the fury in them.

"Why are you doing this?" I ask as his fingers slowly drag down my cheek. Heat coils inside of me as his fingers keep moving. Slowly he slides them into the top of my wet jeans.

"You want to suck me off, Shane? Like old times?" His words are harsh. I want to hide my face from him but he doesn't let me. As soon as I turn my head, his free hand is there grabbing my chin and forcing my gaze back to his. He tilts his head to the side and stares into my eyes.

"Why are you doing this?"

"Doing what? Making you wet?"

"This, Callan," I snap as he keeps his eyes on me. There's an unsettling feeling inside of me, one I can't explain.

"On your knees," he demands. I shouldn't do it. I shouldn't want to but when he steps back and loses his pants, I lose my mind. Like a good girl, I drop to my knees as Callan strokes himself in front of me. I can't pull my eyes away as I lick my lips and wait. He grabs the back of my head and slowly caresses it as he pulls himself closer to me. Then he places the tip on my tongue and I nearly explode. It's been a long time since I've been with Callan. So long that I've missed his touch. He thrusts into my mouth twice before pulling away from me. His pants are up his thighs as I sit on my knees wondering what the hell just happened here. I look up at him through the water that sticks to my lashes as he smirks. That's when I hear it. Chuckles from the side. Turning my head to the left, I see that some of his teammates are watching us. Embarrassment washes over me. My cheeks heat and tears spring to my eyes.

"Get out of here, Shane," Callan growls. I look back at him before shoving myself off the floor of the showers. It takes me seconds to run through the crowd of men and out of the locker room. I don't stop running until I get to the door to head back into the school. Then I lose it. I drop to my knees and sob into my hands when I feel a hand on my shoulder.

"Are you okay?" Luke. It's Luke. He drops down next to me, wrapping his hand around my back as I sob harder. "Why are your clothes wet? Never mind. Come on," he says helping me to my feet. I let him lead me down the sidewalk toward the dorms. I don't know why I go with him but I do. Luke is a good guy. I know he would he never do to me what Callan just did. Maybe that's why I'm so quick to follow him inside. We make it up the stairs when he opens a door and ushers me in.

"I shouldn't be here," I say, softly shivering from the cold water that now clings to me.

"You're soaked. It's fine, Shane. Let me get you something to change into." I watch as Luke moves around the room grabbing some clothes before setting them on the bed. "I'll wait outside." With a quick nod, he leaves the room and I change into his clothes. They're too big but they will be fine to get me home in. I turn to the door and pull it open when Luke turns to face me.

"A little big," he says nodding toward the shirt.

"Thanks for this."

"You want to talk about it?" he asks. I shake my head and wrap my arms around myself.

"It was stupid."

"You look upset still. It wasn't that stupid if it upset you, Shane." God why does he have to be right? Why did he have to see me like this? A new wave of embarrassment hits me as I let my head drop down. Looking at the floor, my chest aches. I love Callan. I think I always have but he's tearing my heart out. Luke's hand comes to my chin, lifting my face so that I'm looking at him.

"Don't do that. Don't let someone else make you feel this way. You don't deserve it," he says softly. My heart leaps into my throat as I look from his eyes to his lips. It's as if he knew what I was thinking and leans in, pressing his lips to mine. There is no explosion when our lips touch. There is no feeling of euphoria like with Callan. It's just… normal. Maybe that's what I need right now. Normal.

Luke pulls back and looks me in the eye. I don't know what to say to him. I don't know what I want to say. If everything could just be this silent, I would be happy. If I never had to face any other bullshit in my life, I would live forever in this moment.

"Are you okay?" he asks when I don't say anything.

"I'm… I don't know what I am anymore, Luke."

"You're Shane McCormick. You're you," he says. Those aren't the words I remember. Callan said them to me once when I felt lost. He said that I was Shane McCormick. The girl that didn't want to be seen but people couldn't help but notice. Oh God. What am I doing?

"I need to go," I say once more, pushing away from him. I head for the door quickly calling out another thank you over my shoulder. It takes me seconds to run down the steps and out the door slamming into someone. Large hands wrap around my shoulders when I look up into two big blue eyes.

"In the men's dorms. What an unpleasant surprise," Knox says keeping a grip on me. His eyes slowly move up and down my body before he raises an eyebrow. "And in someone else's clothes."

"Leave me alone, Knox." I try to move out of his grasp but it does no good.

"Baby brother might not be too happy to know that I saw you here in that," he says nodding toward my clothes.

"Callan has no say in what I do or wear." That gets a laugh out of him. His hands fall away from me, resting at his sides as he smiles.

"You might not think so now but we both know that's a lie," he says.

"You can't be serious? You saw what he did in the locker room."

"What I saw was a girl ready and willing to suck my brother off. That's *all* I saw." The authority in his gaze makes me nervous. I don't like him looking at me like that.

"I wouldn't say shit even if I could." He's afraid I'd tell on Callan for what he did? Who the hell would I tell?

"Which you can't. I mean, what are you going to do? Call Steele? He's the master at this type of game." His words are like a stake to the chest, knocking the air from my lungs.

"I know that all too well. Now leave me alone, Knox." Brushing past him, I hear him chuckle. I don't stop to look back at him or listen to what he has to say. I don't think about it as I walk to my car. Once I'm inside, I let my head fall forward, resting on the steering wheel as soft hot tears stream down my cheeks. I keep my eyes closed, taking deep breaths until I get myself under control.

5
____

CALLAN

I yawn as I kick my feet up on the chair in front of me. I know I said I wanted to finish college but now I'm not so sure. Listening to the asshole at the front of the room talk about business and shit isn't working out for me today. I'm tired, I want to go home. I'm sick of being here. In fact, I'm sick of everything related to this place. Deciding I'd much rather be somewhere else, I shove out of my seat, grab my bag, and head for the door. As soon as I step outside, I see her. Gina? I think that's her name. the girl from the bonfire is walking toward the parking lot. I jog to catch up to her.

"Hey!" She turns when she hears me, a small smile crossing her face.

"Hey, yourself."

"Haven't seen you since the bonfire," I say watching the way her lips curve.

"You haven't been looking hard enough." Ah, she's a playful one.

"Where are you heading right now?" What am I doing?

"Home."

"Care for some company?" This is wrong. I don't want this girl but the thought of having Shane's lips wrapped around my cock won't leave my mind. I let her taste me, one small taste then I pulled away. I don't know what the hell I was thinking having her do that right there when I knew the guys would all walk in. Maybe I wanted to push her buttons the way she does mine. She doesn't see it, in fact, I don't think she knows just how hard she fucking makes me.

"Sure. I'd love some," Gina says batting her lashes at me. I nod and follow her into the parking lot when I see Shane. She's wearing… is that some man's sweatpants? The t-shirt she has on is way too big and her eyes are puffy and red. I know I'm the one that made her cry and I wish I could feel bad for it, but I don't. My eyes follow her when Gina throws her arms around my neck. Her lips are pressing into mine before I can react, her hand cupping my cock like it's a lifeline. I groan into her mouth just as Shane looks over. Her eyes widen as she takes in what's happening. That's when I pull away from Gina. I shouldn't care what Shane thinks. I shouldn't care that she saw that, but I do. Goddamn it, I do.

Shoving Gina back a step, she looks up at me like I've lost my mind and maybe I have but it's Shane's eyes that are haunting me right now.

"What the hell?" Gina snaps until she follows my gaze. "She just came out of Luke's room."

"Luke Norton?" I ask, glancing back at Gina. She nods, licking her lips as I lose it. I storm away from her and straight for the dorms taking the steps two at a time. How dare that little fucker touch her? Who the hell does he think he is? When I'm in front of his door, I start pounding until he opens it.

"Callan? What the hell?" I don't stop to ask questions. I grab the front of his shirt and plow my fist into his face. Luke stumbles and falls back onto the floor when I move for him again. I get a few more good blows in before I'm being pulled off him.

"Yo, Callan. What the fuck man?" Nate, one of my teammates asks looking between the two of us. Anger courses through my veins as I look at Luke.

"You keep your hands off, Shane," I warn him.

"She isn't yours to decide that." Did he just have the balls to say that to me? I step toward him when Nate grabs my shoulder to keep me back.

"I won't warn you twice. If you value your education here, you better stay the fuck away from her," I growl.

"And if I don't? You think I can't get into another school? All three of you Alder assholes treat women like shit. What do you care if I was being nice to her? Clearly you weren't!" I shrug Nate's hand off me and move in again. This time I land a few more hits before Nate shoves me from the room. I look at him, ready to take him on next when he holds his hands up in defeat.

"You might run this school, Alder but he can still press charges. Just calm down," he adds. I nod my head and take a deep breath before turning and jogging down the steps. I'm outside, taking in the fresh air when I hear Whisper.

"Going around kicking people's asses isn't really your style," she says smiling up at me.

"He deserved it. And how the hell do you know already?"

"You just ran out of there and I can see the marks on your hands," she says nodding to my knuckles. I look down and see the bruises already forming as I clench and unclench them.

"He had it coming," I state.

"Did he? Or are you acting like your brothers for another reason?" I want to ignore her, but this is Whisper. She isn't going to go away.

"Shane was wearing his clothes. Gina saw her come out of his room."

"Gina? As in slut Gina? Gina that will hike her skirt up for anyone with a cock? That Gina?" Okay, I get her point. Whisper rolls her eyes and I can't stop the smile that crosses my face. Tossing my arm around her shoulder, I pull her into my side.

"Want to get drunk?"

"God, I thought you would never ask. Your brother has been hiding the liquor bottles." She laughs.

"From you?" I ask looking down at her by my side.

"Yeah. Apparently, I'm frisky when I'm drunk." She rolls her eyes once more.

"I don't think so. I think you have to let go every once in a while, right? If not, you might lose your mind."

"Is that what you were doing back there?" she asks, tucking her arm around my waist.

"Something like that."

"You love her?"

"I don't know anymore, Whisper."

"Yes, you do. It's not a trick question, Callan. Obviously, you loved her at some point, right?"

"It was high school. I don't think you can consider that love," I tell her.

"Sure, you can. If that's what you felt. You can't let something you love get away, Callan. You just can't." The sadness in her tone causes me to flinch. I don't like sadness in her. She deserves more than that.

"You're happy aren't you, Whisper?" She stops walking and moves to stand in front of me, her hands on her hips.

"Are you turning this around on me?" she asks, her eyebrow raised and ready.

"No. I'm just asking you."

"I love Steele, Callan. I don't think I've ever loved anyone in my life, but I love him."

"How do you know?"

"Well, I hate when he isn't near me. I hate the feeling I get in my stomach when he leaves. When I wake up, I think about him. When I go to sleep, he's all I dream about. Steele and I don't have some kind of conventional love story, Callan. I can't explain what it does to me when he's a dick. It makes me feel… loved." I know she loves my brother. I know how she feels about all of us, but I can't decide how I feel about Shane. I trust Whisper's instincts when it comes to people. Hell she was spot on about us.

"I've looked into her more in-depth lately," I tell her.

"What do you mean?"

"Just what I said! I looked into her. She has secrets, Whisper. One's that I never fucking saw coming. I don't know how to bring it up or how to walk away from them."

"You don't bring them up. You let her tell you at her own pace, Callan. You should know better than anyone that you can't force those things on people. We'll break." The softness in her eyes says it all. I know I shouldn't push her, but this is something else. Something more than any of us would have ever thought.

"You don't get it, Whisper. What I found out… I can't look at her the same way anymore."

"What the hell did you find out, Callan? What's so bad that you can't look at her the same?" I wish I could tell her. I want to tell her, but I also know Whisper. I know her history and I know mine. Neither of us want to bring this up and dwell on it. Instead of telling her anything, I grab her and pull her into me.

"What am I going to do?" I ask softly.

"I don't know because you won't tell me the problem," she responds.

"I can't give you that part. I'm sorry but I can't." She squeezes me back and sighs into my chest.

"Then I can't help you. When you're ready, you know I'm here."

"Thanks. I know that much. I just need to see what the fuck else is happening that I don't know about first. If there's one secret, there are usually more."

"Your family knows all about that!" I release her and laugh a little. She's not wrong. This family was built on secrets and lies. Nothing we learn about my dad really shocks me anymore.

"That we do but at least we have you now," I tell her. She laughs, throwing her head back as she smiles.

"Yeah, that was the best prize of all. The homeless jackass."

"You aren't a jackass. You're just you, Whisper. We wouldn't want you any other way."

"You say it like we're in a harem." Now it's my turn to laugh.

"Are you opposed?"

"Ha! Not a chance in hell. Your brother would kill us all."

"He didn't kill us in that pool house," I tease.

"Do you still think about that?"

"Your hot little body on full display for all of us. The way your tits tasted on my tongue," I say huskily. A moan escapes her lips as I laugh.

"Now who's thinking about it?"

"Damn it, Callan! Now I'm going to have to go home and get myself off."

"Why? Where's Steele?" I ask holding the car door open for her and allowing her to climb in.

"Some stupid meeting," she grumbles.

"Well, you can watch me rub one out then. I don't think he cares if you watch," I quip.

"You're sick. Take me home."

6

SHANE

"How long are we going to do this, Mom?" She looks up at me with sad eyes. That should be enough for me but it isn't. We don't need this. I don't need this.

"It's not that easy, Shane. How do you think you got into that school?"

"So, he gets to treat us like shit so that I can go to school? I'm sick of it, Mom. I'm sick of all of it. This has been going on for years and I'm sorry but it's getting old." Admitting that to her took a lot of guts. I know that my mom seems to love Matt and I wish I could say the same, but I can't. My stepdad, Matt, is an abusive piece of shit. Then again so is my mom. If she wasn't drunk off her ass right now, I wouldn't even be talking to her like this. This is the only time I can speak my mind without having to worry about the punishment that would follow.

"Getting old? Shut the hell up, Shane. You have everything handed to you on a silver platter. Ever since Matt came into our lives, you've had it all," she sneers. This is bullshit. She can't think that can she? She knows what happened to me! She knows because she made it all disappear!

"This is bullshit. I can't be here," I say shoving out of my chair. I start toward the door when Matt walks in. Speak of the devil and he appears.

"Where are you off to in such a hurry?"

"Out."

"It's almost ten at night. You aren't going anywhere," he says stepping closer to me. I take a deep breath, ready for a fight when I make my move. I rush past him and out the door, running down the driveway when I hear him.

"Keep running! You will never be allowed back here!" Thank God for small miracles. When I'm far enough away from the house, I slow down to catch my breath. Each step I take in the darkness is one I can't come back from. Not that I really want to but where the hell am I going to go? What am I going to do now? I have some money, not a lot, but I have saved up what I've made from working at the dance studio although they just opened not long ago.

Tears burn the back of my eyes as I walk into the old town square. Sitting on the small bench, I rest my head in my hands. Should I apologize? Should I go back and beg for forgiveness? No. I can't do that. Not after everything else that's happened between the three of us. I won't do it. Instead, I pull my phone out and dial Whisper before quickly hanging up. She will tell Callan. Then what? What happens after that? Finally letting the tears fall down my cheeks, I sigh. I don't know what to do. Would Steele even let me come there? Just for the night?

"What are you doing here?" I nearly jump out of my own skin when I hear someone speak. The small startled scream that left my mouth was unexpected.

"Jesus, Luke." I press my hand to my chest trying to slow the beating of my heart. He scared the shit out of me.

"Sorry. I was out jogging. What are you doing out here?"

"I needed some air."

"You want me to walk you home?" he offers.

"No. I'm good. I'm just going to call Whisper and see if she wants to hang out," I say quickly. A strange feeling slips under my skin as I watch him shift from foot to foot. Luke's never made me feel uncomfortable until right now. I slide my phone out as he watches me.

"I'll hang out with you, if you want," he offers as I bring the phone to my ear.

"That's okay." *Please pick up, Whisper.*

"Hello?"

"Hey! What are you doing?" I ask happily when she answers yet never take my eyes off Luke.

"Sleeping. What's going on?"

"Oh yeah? So, I'm down at the old square. I was wondering if you wanted to come hang out for a while." *Please pick up on the signs, Whisper.*

"That's dangerous, Shane. What the hell is going on?"

"So, you want to come?"

"I'm on my way." The line goes dead but I keep talking. Something evil lurks in the air, but I can't place it.

"Really? Yeah, that sounds like fun."

"Shane?" Luke says pulling my attention to him. "I'm gonna go." Nodding, I watch him walk away as I laugh to myself at something the pretend Whisper is saying. This goes on for at least another ten minutes when I see headlights. Car doors slam when Knox is running toward me.

"What the hell is going on?" he asks looking around the town square. That's when I lose it. I break down and crumble. Sobs rip from my throat as I fall to my knees. Whisper's there in no time, wrapping her arms around me.

"Who was it? Who was here?"

"Luke, but he didn't do anything. It was just… I had this creepy feeling while he was here," I admit.

"Where did he go?" Knox asks, his hands balling at his sides.

"I don't know. When he knew Whisper was coming, he left." Whisper helps me off the ground and pulls me into her side as she leads me to the car. I'm thankful when I get there that Callan isn't inside. Whisper helps me in as Knox looks around.

"Why are you even out here? What's going on?"

"I can't go home, Whisper. I just can't." More tears. I hate tears. I hate feeling weak and useless.

"Fine. You're staying with me."

"You don't think you should run that by your man?" Knox asks climbing in the driver's seat.

"No, I don't think I have to run it by anyone. I live there too, Knox, and I said she could stay," she snaps.

"I don't want any trouble, Whisper. I just… I just need someplace for tonight. I'll figure it all out tomorrow."

"You're staying as long as you need to. I don't care what Steele has to say about it," she says.

"It's not Steele I'm worried about," Knox chimes in from the front.

"I'll stay out of his way. I promise. I just want to sleep, anyway."

The car ride back to the house is silent. Whisper rubs my hand where she held it in hers but all I can think about is what I was going to do now. Where I'm going to go. I should have planned this out better. I didn't plan on staying gone forever, just for the night. Yet again, I was stupid. I didn't think.

I climb out of the car when Knox opens the door, ushering us inside. I remember this place from when Callan and I dated in high school. It looks exactly the same.

"You can stay in Dad's old room. It's a little messy but none of us will be going in there," Knox says before walking away.

"I shouldn't be here," I whisper under my breath.

"You're my friend. You should be here. I don't know what's happening but clearly you needed space. Now you have it. Come on," she says leading me up the stairs and down the hall. Once we're inside the room, I collapse onto the bed.

"I'll find you something to wear," Whisper says as she leaves the room. I take a deep breath, begging myself not to cry again. I don't know what I'm going to do but being out of that house sure does feel right.

7
———

CALLAN

Steele laughs as we stumble back into the house. After his bullshit meeting, we met up for a few drinks. Which turned into a few more.

"I'm going to get my dick sucked," he says as we make our way up the stairs.

"She's going to cut that fucker off if she knows you were out drinking all night," I remind him.

"She won't. She loves it too much." His laughter echoes off the walls as he stumbles toward his room. The hall sways, the walls moving left and right. My head spins as I make my way down the hall. Falling into the last room, I chuckle under my breath.

"You fucked up everything. Everything!" I roar as I stand in his room. I can't believe he's gone. I can't believe we killed him. It was always going to happen but now? Now I want answers from a man that can't give them.

"You were a selfish bastard. Always caring more about you

than anyone else." My words are slurred but I don't care. I need to say them. I need him to hear them in the depths of hell.

"Callan?"

"Oh shit! Are you a ghost? Ghost dad?" I laugh to myself when the light on the table flips on. I blink my eyes against the harsh light when I see her. Long blonde hair hanging around her perfectly heart-shaped face.

"Are you okay?" she asks.

"Are you sleeping with ghost dad?" I ask not really understanding what I'm saying.

"What? What are you talking about?" She throws the blankets back and climbs out of the bed, her long legs bare and exposed.

"You are sleeping with ghost dad!" Anger mixes with the alcohol in my veins as I think about it. How could she?

"How much did you drink, Callan?" she asks coming toward me.

"Not enough, apparently."

"Your dad is dead, Cal."

"Yeah, no shit. Who do you think killed him?" She gasps and I know I fucked up.

"What the hell is the screaming about?" Knox's voice filters through the room. I turn my head to look at him and then smile.

"She's fucking ghost dad," I slur.

"You're an idiot. A drunk idiot." That came from Knox. Shane giggles when my eyes move back to find her. I let my gaze slip over her tone body. From her bare legs to one of Whisper's t-shirts.

"You laughed. You haven't laughed in a long time, Shane." Her bright eyes slowly fade back into the nothingness that I've seen in her for a long time now. And I know why.

"Let's get you to your room," Knox says, grabbing my wrist and tugging me. I turn on him, ready to fight.

"Don't touch me! The only one I want touching me is her," I growl pointing in her direction. I'm lucky I'm drunk and have no idea what the hell I'm saying right now. Sober me would not be doing this but that's the difference between drunk me. He thinks this is a great idea.

"She doesn't want to touch you. Come on, Cal." Knox tries again when I shove him away.

"She doesn't? You don't want to touch me, Shane?" Turning back to her, I see the way she looks at me. Or maybe it's my drunken mind that thinks she's looking at me like I'm her next meal.

"Callan, go to sleep. This isn't you," Shane says shocking me a little. I stumble toward her, struggling with the way the room is spinning. When I'm close enough to her, I reach up and cup her cheek. Something in the back of my mind is telling me this is all wrong but I can't think of why. So I don't stop. I let my fingers run down her cheek, caressing her as her eyes slowly fall closed.

"Yeah, she wants to touch me."

"Let's go, Callan," Knox says once more.

"Will you take me?" I ask Shane, softly. Her eyes dance between mine, an unsure look crosses her face.

"Fine. Come on."

"You don't have to do this, Shane," Knox chimes in.

"You can shut up anytime, brother! She loves me! This is what people do for the one's they love," I remind him even though that doesn't sound right leaving my lips. Shane rolls her eyes and grabs my arm leading me from the room.

"I got him. It's fine," she says over her shoulder as she half drags me down the hall. All of my senses are on high alert. I can smell her. I can nearly taste her on the tip of my tongue.

Shane leads me into my room and straight toward the bed. When she tries to sit me on the edge, I wrap my arms around her waist and pull her down with me.

"Stop, Callan," she says, although she doesn't sound like she means it.

"I just want to hold you, Shane. Just let me hold you, okay?"

"We can't do this," she says softly.

"You smell so damn good." She does. It's not a lie. I could breathe her in forever and never get tired of her smell.

"I need to go, Callan."

"No." The word came out as a growl. She doesn't fight me. Did I scare her? Why do I like the sound of that so much? Damn, I'm beyond drunk.

"Why do you need me here?" she asks in nearly a whisper.

"I know all your secrets, Shane." She tenses as I roll onto my side so that we are face to face. Maybe I'm an asshole or maybe drunk me just needs to push her but I keep going. My hand slowly slides down her side until I reach the hem of her shirt. When my hand touches her flesh, she jerks. God, I've missed that feeling. Touching her. Sliding my hand under the thin fabric, I let it run up her side to the swell of her breast.

"You need to stop this, Callan. You're drunk. You don't know what you're doing right now."

"I know what I'm doing. I know what you did too." I remind her of the secret I hold.

"I didn't do anything," she says, trying to push me off her.

"Oh, you did. And I know. You let someone else slip in between these thighs, Shane. How could you do that?" I roll so that I'm on top of her, nuzzling my face into her neck.

"Not since you, Callan. Please just stop this." Is she begging? Fuck, I like when she begs. My cock hardens even more than it was, listening to her beg.

"Not since me?" I ask pulling back so I can look down at her. She shakes her head as tears spring to her eyes. "Why?"

"I didn't want anyone else."

"You were waiting for me?"

"It's not like that, Callan. I knew we were done," she says softly.

"We're never done, Shane. We will never ever be done." The groan that rips from my throat startles her. I run my hand back down her side, grabbing her panties in my hand and jerking. When I can't get them to move, I sit up and rip them from her body.

"Stop, Callan. You're going to regret this," she says, trying to push away from me. Not a chance in hell. I don't care what she thinks I will regret. I won't. I want her.

"Not a chance in hell," I growl pulling at my jeans. I kick them off my legs and lose my boxers along with them before I'm right back between her legs. Pressing my lips to hers, she's hesitant. She doesn't kiss me back and that pisses me off. Jerking my head back, I stare at her. I look right into her eyes as I grab my cock and slide inside of her.

"Callan," she cries. Not a good cry either. It's sad. I don't want to make her sad.

"You're so beautiful. I thought you would be my wife one day," I tell her as I thrust inside of her. Tears fall down her cheeks as she watches me. Fuck, she feels so good. It's like I was made to be inside of her. Shane is everything.

"Stop." I shake my head.

"You don't want that. You want me, Shane. I can feel you," I whisper before pressing my lips to hers. When she turns her head, I stop moving.

"You let him inside of you. You let him inside and then… God how could you do that?" I roar in her face. The secrets out or at least part of it is. Her face transforms into something I've never seen before. Her hands shove at me, trying to get me to move as she cries harder.

"I told you I knew your secrets. How could you? With him of all people, Shane." My own cries mean nothing as my cock decides now is a good time to finish. I come inside of her, my tears mixing with hers. I rest my face in her neck as we both cry.

"Let me go," she says softly.

"I wish I could."

"Please," she cries as my eyes slowly flutter closed.

"Stay with me."

8
____

SHANE

I can smell him on my skin even after the third shower. Whisper has tried to get me to talk but I have nothing to say. I don't know that I would tell her if I could. He knows and I don't know how he knows but he does. The question is will he remember what happened last night when he's sober?

I pick at my bacon as I look around the room. Steele is hungover as hell and Knox just looks unfazed by any of it. Maybe this is their normal these days. It was never like this before. I remember staying over and their dad having the maid make breakfast. We would all sit in complete silence and eat. Then his dad would excuse himself.

"We're going to Intensity tonight. You're coming," Whisper says pointing her fork at me.

"I can't dance."

"Everyone can dance. You just have to let yourself feel," Knox says.

"Maybe I don't want to feel." His eyes slowly move up to meet mine before he nods his understanding. Maybe going wouldn't be so bad. I do love music and Whisper has been teaching me some dance moves.

"Fine. I'm in."

"Good. It'll be fun," Steele states. Callan strolls into the room looking like sex on a stick and I shift in my seat remembering him inside of me last night. He looks up, his eyes moving across everyone but skipping me. I don't know why I expected anything else.

"What's for breakfast?" he asks, scratching at his stomach. I can't help but look at the trail of dark hair that disappears into his jeans. Damn that makes my mouth go dry. I grab my juice and take a drink trying to recover when Callan sits next to me. I sigh knowing that he had no other choice.

"You sleep well?" Whisper asks staring right at him. She's a little pissed. She might have heard me crying in the shower and asked me what happened. I didn't tell her everything, just the basics.

"Yeah. Why?" God, he doesn't even remember. Embarrassment hits me hard. My cheeks heat as I look anywhere but at him. Thank God someone knocks on the door breaking the weird tension in the room. Steele shoves out of his seat and heads for the door as Whisper stares Callan down.

"Are you really going to sit there and act like that?" she snaps in his direction. My eyes move from her to him and back. Why is she doing this? I know we're friends but damn.

"It meant nothing," he says through his clenched jaw. A gasp slips free and I'm on my feet ready to rush from the room when he's behind me.

"Shane." He says my name with longing and anger mixed in one. His fingers intertwine with mine and my heart melts a little more.

"Hey guys. You're not going to believe this shit!" Steele's

voice is angry as he walks back into the room followed by a woman and a little girl.

"Who the hell is she?" Knox asks, looking up from his spot at the table. Callan shifts, tugging me with him before moving away from the woman. It's almost as if he can sense something is off about her.

"What's going on?" Whisper asks.

"This lady claims to be our mom," Steele says, snickering a little.

"She's dead. Our mom is dead," Callan states, although the way he tightens his fingers around mine says otherwise.

"I'm not, Callan. It's true. I'm your mom," the woman says. Risking a glance at Callan, I see the way his jaw tics.

"This doesn't make sense. Dad said our mom was dead," Knox snaps shoving out of his chair. His eyes never leave hers as he takes her in. I knew this part of their lives. Their mom died when Callan was only one. I remember him telling me about how hard it was for him not knowing her or seeing her. Not having a woman around to help raise him. It hurt something deep inside of him.

"There's a lot that you boys don't know. I'd like the chance to tell you," she says. She's beautiful. Tall with dark hair, much like the boys. They don't look like her though, they look like their dad.

"We don't know who the hell you are. What makes you think we would believe you anyway?" Steele asks crossing his arms over his chest.

"I'm your mother, Steele. My God, I can't believe you are all grown up."

"If you are really our mom, where the hell have you been all our lives?" Callan snaps. His fingers loosen around mine before he slips them away completely. He mimics his brother's stance, crossing his arms over his chest.

"That's a long story. One I'd love the chance to share with you."

"Why the hell should they let you in? Huh? You left them when they were kids!" Whisper yells. She stands and moves up next to Steele almost in a protective manner. It makes my heart happy for him, that he has that. They all grew up in such an unconventional way and they didn't get the love and protection that a child deserves so to see at least one of them getting it now is amazing.

"I didn't have a choice."

"Who's the kid?" Knox asks looking down at her. Everyone's gaze follows as the little girl slinks back to hide behind the woman.

"This is Bella. I adopted her when she was a baby. Can you say hi, Bella?" The woman taps her shoulder and motions toward all of us. She looks to be maybe around three or four. Her big blue eyes move between all of us before she says hi. This is weird. It's awkward and the tension in the air isn't going anywhere.

"What name were you living under? It sure as hell hasn't been Carol Alder," Steele snaps. Everyone turns their heads to look at him wondering what he's talking about and how he'd know that.

"You're right."

"Wait. How the fuck would you know?" Knox asks him.

"Things Dad would say wouldn't add up. I thought, no, I prayed she was out there somewhere. That she didn't die and just leave us to this shit but the more I searched, the less I came up with. Carol Alder was dead."

"So who the hell are you?" Callan asks this time. The room becomes even thicker with tension.

"Whisper, take Bella to get something to eat. We need to talk," Steele says. Whisper nods and moves toward the little girl, grabbing her hand in hers. Bella willingly goes as Carol watches with a slight smile on her face. That's when all eyes shoot to me. I start to take a step away when Callan grabs my wrist and pulls me back.

"Stay with me." I don't know why he wants me here and frankly I'm not comfortable staying but for some stupid reason I do. I nod my head and follow him back to the table and sit next to him. Everyone takes their seats as they look to Carol for answers.

"Start talking," Steele says holding so much authority in his tone. I've never heard him like that before.

"You sound a lot like your father right now."

"We aren't here to talk about him. Spit it out or get the hell out of our house!"

9

———

CALLAN

We're heading out for the night now that Carol is gone but the thoughts still linger. Her story could be true. Let's be honest, my dad was a shady piece of shit that got what he wanted, no questions asked. Carol said that he ran her off, had her on so many drugs that she couldn't think straight. She said he told her that she was weak and would only ruin us boys so he sent her away. She was a drug addict for most of the time she was gone. She said after she got clean, she adopted Bella and waited for the right opportunity to show up here which happened to be after Dad was dead. I couldn't dispute that. If what she said was true, I wouldn't want to come back either if he was still around.

"We aren't talking about this tonight," Steele says once more after Knox keeps on. Walking into Intensity, we all need to let off some steam. I know for sure I do. My night was a mess. This morning was worse. I fucked her. Even through her tears I took what I shouldn't have. I let her know that I knew her secrets and then this morning I ran from the house after Carol left. I couldn't look at her knowing what I know.

"Thank God. I'm pretty over this shit already," I chime in. I don't know what I feel. I don't know how to respond to what she said. Is it possible? Of course it is. Growing up the way we have will tell you that. Nothing is impossible in our world.

Music echoes off the walls as we make our way through the crowd. Leddy finds us easily and comes to say hi. She hugs Steele, flips off Knox and winks in my direction. That's when I notice Whisper and Shane heading our way. Whisper smiles, at peace with being here but Shane doesn't. Rage is something I'm becoming used to. Rage and anger at her. Why? I couldn't tell you, but I feel it. I want to hurt her, I want to see her break, and then some sick part of me wants to put her back together but my life is a mess. Everything in it is a mess. I don't need Shane around right now but as soon as I see her start to dance, I know I want to torture her. Grabbing the first girl I find, I drag her out into the middle of the room. All eyes are on us.

"Who are you making jealous?" the girl hollers over the music. I shake my head and she smirks. She can feel it. The way the air thickens around us. Grabbing her by the back of the neck, I pull her body against mine and grind on her. Then I shove her forward, forcing her ass up and into my hands. I let them roam over the soft globes as my eyes find Shane's. Her lips part and I can see the hurt in her eyes. Too bad for her. Pulling the girl back up, I spin her around, shoving her down in front of me. She grips my hips and rolls her head before popping back up and throwing her arms around my neck. We keep moving like this until the song changes and someone else wants the floor. The girl doesn't stop though. Instead, she leans in, running her tongue up my neck as chills race through me. We're close enough to Shane that I can see every reaction she has. Just when I think she's about to run, I smirk. That smirk doesn't stay in place long. She grabs Knox and pulls him into her, pressing her body against his. He moves to grab her hips, grinding against her. I know this is all for show but that doesn't mean it doesn't piss me off. I shouldn't want her. She's a liar.

"You're going to lose her forever," Whisper yells over the music.

"I never had her. She's a liar," I remind her. She rolls her eyes and goes back to dancing as I watch the two of them. I can't believe she's doing this with my brother of all people. Turning on my heel, I head toward the bathrooms when I feel hands wrap around my waist. I know that touch. Dragging Shane around in front of me, I slam her against the wall.

"What the hell are you doing?"

"You fucked me last night."

"Yeah, I did. So what? It meant nothing," I remind her. I watch her swallow hard, but she keeps her head held high.

"It meant nothing to me either," she says. She's lying again. I can see the look in her eyes. I step into her space, ready to play her game. Reaching up, I cup her cheek in my hand watching the way she slowly releases her breath.

"Is that what you want? You want me to fuck you, no strings attached?" What the hell am I doing? This isn't me. This isn't what I want.

"I want you anyway I can have you, Callan." That… That is the most real thing she's ever said to me. I lean in, pressing my lips to hers. The taste of her on my tongue has my body wound tightly. The way she lets my tongue sweep into her mouth has my cock hard and ready for her. Even with all the other bullshit going on in my life, this is something I remember. Her. I will always remember her.

I growl when I grab her hips and lift her in my arms. We're in the bathroom, I'm kicking the door closed and locking it in seconds. Setting her on her feet, I drop to my knees and push her skirt up. Trailing my fingers along her panties, she moans lightly. That's what I wanted to hear. Hooking my finger in her panties, I slip them down and help her step out of them before shoving them in my pocket. Then I lean in, inhaling her. Her hands come to rest in my hair, tugging lightly. My tongue slowly sweeps over her and she gasps. It's been years since I've tasted her. Years since she's been this open to me. Spreading her lips wide, I dive in and take charge. I lick, suck, and tug on her clit before starting all over. Shane's body trembles when I dip my tongue inside of her just to start over once more. She's gasping, moaning and panting for more.

"Cal. Shit!" she hisses when I toy with her clit. A little harder, a little faster. Shane explodes as I lap it all up. I knew she would taste good. I remember her taste. I used to make her come over and over with my tongue when all she wanted was my cock buried deep inside of her. I pull back and stand, adjusting myself as I move. When I'm standing in front of her, she reaches for me. Grabbing her wrists, I pin them above her head as I get into her space.

"You want me, Shane?" I ask gruffly. She licks her lips and fuck; do I want them wrapped around my cock.

"Yes," she says huskily.

"Too bad. You can't have me. You took away something I wanted with you and only you. You ruined everything with your lies, Shane." She starts to open her mouth but I don't let her. I silence her with mine. A kiss that's more punishing than anything I could say to her. When I stop, her lips are swollen and bruised. Just the way I like them.

"I'm sorry, Callan. You don't understand what happened." Grabbing her face roughly in my hands, I force her to look at me.

"What don't I understand? That you lied? That you fucked your stepdad?" That must have stung. She pushes me back and slaps me across the face as I laugh.

"You don't know anything!" she screams before turning and rushing from the bathroom.

10

SHANE

I'm not sure what I feel as I sit here and watch Whisper dancing around the room. She has her drink in her hand, laughing and smiling. I know parts of her past but for the most part, she keeps it to herself. Just the way I planned to keep mine. Now Callan knows. I don't know why he looked into me. I don't know why he cared, yet here we are. I'm homeless, sitting in the Alder's living room. I never pictured this but here I am.

"Why are you being so pissy?" Knox asks as he drops on to the couch next to me.

"I'm not. I feel like I'm imposing," I say, honestly. Knox throws his arm around my shoulder, his hand resting on my breast like it belongs there.

"You are imposing." His words sting but his fingers move. Grabbing my nipple through my shirt, I gasp and try to move. Knox keeps me in place, tugging at my nipple.

"Stop!" I scream catching everyone's attention. Steele glances over and smirks at what his brother is doing when Callan looks up. Fire dances in those big blue eyes of his, flickering with every twist of his brother's fingers.

"Having a little fun, brother?" Callan asks while his eyes stay on mine.

"I figured Whisper shouldn't be the only one that got in on this," Knox adds. My eyes flash to Whisper's as she laughs. I try to brush Knox's hand away once more, but he doesn't stop. When I'm about to stand, Callan moves. He's next to me in seconds, pressing me back into the couch.

"Is that what you want? You want us all to touch you? Fuck you with our fingers, our mouths?" The way he says it sounds evil. I look up at him, directly into his eyes when he sees it. Then he moves. He pushes Knox's hand away from me before standing and walking away, and I'm back to being alone. Knox chuckles but doesn't move his arm. Instead he pulls me closer, running his lips down the side of my neck.

"Stop, please," I whisper as tears fill my eyes.

"Why? You want it, Shane. You want him." I turn my head to look at Knox. He knows I want his brother. Swallowing hard, maybe Knox is right. Maybe this is the only way to get Callan to really notice me. I nod my head and Knox moves. He lifts me onto his lap so that I'm facing him. His lips claim my neck as his own. I can't say that it doesn't feel good, it does but I know it's not right. Even as his lips move to my shoulder. Even when he bites into my flesh. An audible gasp leaves my lips as I feel his cock harden beneath me. The couch shifts and Callan is there. Watching. Music pumps through the speakers as Knox keeps going. He grabs my hips, holding me against his hard-on while grinding me against him. God, it feels so damn good but Callan's eyes are punishing. I watch as he pulls his cock out of his jeans and strokes it in front of me. Whisper laughs, Steele growls but no one says a word as whatever this is, happens. Each breath I take is strangled. My body is humming with so much energy I can barely stand it. That's when Callan growls. He reaches over and pulls me off Knox's lap before ripping my shorts down my legs. I'm back in his lap, straddling him when he lowers me down on his cock.

"Cal!" I cry out his name as he pumps into me.

"Grab his cock!" he demands. I look over at Knox as he strokes his own cock. When I don't move, Callan does. He thrusts his hips upward causing me to cry out. Then he reaches up and grabs my hand, placing it on Knox's cock. Heat spirals inside of me as I ride Callan and rub Knox. I notice both of them groan and lean their heads back on the couch when someone comes up behind us. I don't turn to look but when a hand reaches around and plucks my nipple roughly, I explode. As I come, Steele's warm breath dances over my flesh.

"Yeah, we knew you'd like it," he whispers before pressing a soft kiss to my neck. When he moves, my head drops onto Callan's shoulder. His cock pulses inside of me as he fills me. He grunts as he comes but his hands never move from my hips. In fact, they tighten.

"How is it you always seem to end up on my cock?" he asks as he tries to catch his breath. Pain slices through me as his fingers dig into my flesh. A soft whimper escapes me as tears burn the back of my eyes.

"If the sex fest is over, Carol is coming over," Steele announces.

"Carol, the missing piece of the Alder puzzle," Whisper slurs.

"Fuck her," Callan roars, shoving me off him. I nearly fall on my ass when Whisper is in his face.

"You know what, Callan? I'm sick of you fucking her and then shoving her to the side. You need to decide what the hell it is you want. You can't keep using her like this!" Her anger makes my heart leap. She knows how hard this is for me. This push and pull between us is ripping me apart. Callan shoves to his feet, shoving his cock back into his jeans as he looks at her.

"This has nothing to do with you."

"Really? She's my best friend, Callan! My only friend!" Steele moves now as I pull my shorts up my legs.

"Stay out of it, Whisper," he orders her. Her head whips around, her eyes narrowing on his. Oh, this isn't good. Not at all.

"Excuse me?"

"You heard me," he says crossing his arms over his chest.

"You don't own me, Steele. Don't you dare tell me not to stand up for her."

"I don't need you to," I say softly.

"You aren't her keeper," he challenges.

"Neither is Callan."

"I don't need any of you!" I scream, catching everyone's attention. All heads turn my way when I lose it. Tears spring to my eyes as I shake my head and try to roughly wipe them away.

"I'm sorry, Shane," Whisper says stepping toward me, but I raise my hand to stop her.

"Don't. I don't need this. I don't need you to stand up for me. I don't need you to care about me." With those words my eyes find Callan's. He opens his mouth but he doesn't say anything. He just watches me. Waiting. Waiting for what? Me to break? I'm done breaking. I'm tired of falling apart over a man that doesn't really want me.

"Shane," Whisper says. I huff out a breath and turn on my heel heading for the door. Grabbing my purse and slipping my feet into my shoes I walk out. I have to. I need to get away from them. But where am I going?

There are many things in life that I can handle but seeing the hatred in Callan's eyes isn't one of them. My heart crumbles as I realize that he will never look at me with that sweet smile he has. He will never hold me and promise me forever. As I keep walking, I let the tears fall when I end up back where I started. Looking up at the two-story house, I sigh. This, this is what my life is.

Stepping in the front door, the negative energy hits me hard. This house is full of lies and anger, and I hate being a part of it.

"You came back." My mom's voice drifts from the living room. Instead of going to my room, I walk into the living room and find her on the couch with a cup of coffee in her hand.

"Should I leave?" She shakes her head and pats the seat next to her. Me and my mom aren't close. We never have been and after what happened to me, no, after what she let happen to me I never wanted to be near her again. Nevertheless, I walk over and sit on the edge of the couch. There it is. The marks on her face that I knew would be there.

"When will it stop?"

"Never. It will never stop. There are so many things you don't know, Shane."

"Like what?"

"Like the fact that I will ruin you. Or the fact that I have my own plans for that piece of shit Alder family." Matt's voice burns through my body like acid.

"Like you could stand against them," I sneer. I shouldn't have said it, but I need to stand up for myself. I'm sick of letting people walk all over me. That's when I feel it. The burn in my scalp as I'm jerked from the couch by my hair. I scream right before I'm tossed into the wall where I thud and fall to the floor. Instead of letting the tears fall, I laugh. Taking a page of Whisper's book, I harden myself to the assholes that want to hurt me.

11

CALLAN

"Drugs? That's what you're going with?" I ask as I look Carol in the eye. I don't remember my mom. Never saw a picture of her in my life so it's not like I'd know what she looks like but I can see it. The blue eyes, the dark hair. We didn't just get that from our dad. She's beautiful. Still doesn't make sense though.

"When I was sent away, I was kept in a room. They pumped me full of drugs, Callan. I didn't know what day it was let alone how to get away. The times I did try to run, I didn't make it far. I was addicted to whatever they shoved in my veins." Her eyes fill with tears as she looks between us. Knox is the calmest of the three which is odd.

"You realize just how this sounds to us don't you?" Steele asks, shifting in his seat. He's uncomfortable, just like the rest of us.

"I do and I'm sorry. I wanted you boys. More than I wanted my own life, but your father wouldn't allow it."

"Why did he wait and have Knox and Callan?" Steele asks.

"He needed to make sure that if one didn't want this role, the other would," she says. It makes sense.

"Jesus Christ," I whisper. It hits me. Like a fucking brick to the chest. The fights. His men. That's why he was always so hard on Steele. He wasn't trying to punish him; he was trying to kill him. My hands clench in my lap as I shove out of my seat.

"Cal?" Knox says my name, but I don't listen.

"That was it, wasn't it?" My question is directed at Steele and he knows it.

"I didn't realize at first," he says softly, looking the other way. That's when I move. I grab him and jerk him out of his seat. Anger filters through my veins as I pull my first back and swing. It connects with his jaw barely fazing him. He doesn't stumble back, just looks at me. He reminds me of him. Our dad. So fucking stoic and put together. Steele is probably the most put together of all of us.

"You knew. You knew he was out for blood and you took it every single time! Why?"

"Dad knew I didn't want this shit. He knew I didn't want to run the businesses for him."

"What changed? You're running it now?" I ask needing to know the answer.

"Everything changed. He's gone. This is us now. Not him. Us!" he growls shoving me back a step.

"He could have had you killed," I remind him.

"But he didn't. I'm here. We are here!"

"This is bullshit. All of it. He's gone, so what the fuck is it you want?" Knox asks, causing us all to look his way. His eyes are on her. Our mom. "Money? Is that it? You want us to pay you what he owed?"

"No. Of course not. I want my family back. I want my sons,"

she says. Something about her isn't right. She's too… sincere for a woman that should be bitter and angry.

"I don't like this," I ponder.

"I don't know what else you want me to say, Callan. My God! Your father was a real piece of work. He wanted things the way he wanted them and that was that. I'm sure he was just as bad when you were growing up," she snaps showing her true colors. She makes me uncomfortable. There's an aura around her that I don't like.

"I'm out of here," I say, turning on my heel. I hurry out of the room when Whisper stops me.

"Hey, Callan."

"What?" I ask spinning to face her. I don't need her shit too. I don't trust Carol and that's that.

"I love you."

"Why are you saying that?" She steps into me, her arms going around my waist like they usually do.

"Because you need to hear it from someone that means it," she adds. I sigh and wrap my arms around her.

"You feel it?" I ask her softly, pressing my lips into the top of her hair.

"She's evil, Cal. They don't see it."

"You can," I tell her. I know she can. Whisper came from evil, she knows when she sees it.

"I'm sorry."

"Don't be. I'm glad I'm not the only one that feels it," I tell her. She nods her head and pulls away from me without another word. I turn and head out the door and jog down the stairs until I'm on the sidewalk. Then I run.

Running has always cleared my head. Although it hasn't been working lately, I have to stay in shape for football. It's weird without the guys with me. This is our thing. We all go when one goes. I guess that's what it means to grow up and grow apart. Me and my brothers are still close but we all seem to be branching off into our own lives lately. Not that I didn't want that or see it coming, it's just hard to get used to. Our lives have always been one. We did what we were told, what was expected of us. I suppose that's what is slowly tearing us apart too.

My breathing comes in bursts as I race down the road. I don't think, just run, until I stop in front of her house. What it is about her that draws me in? Why can't I seem to keep away from her? I'm about to turn and run when I hear someone scream. Instead of running away, I'm dashing up the stairs. I take them two at a time before kicking the door in. That's when I see it. Matt, Shane's stepdad, has her mom on the ground beating her but something else feels off. Something else is wrong.

"Get off her!" I roar, catching his attention.

"You. Fuck you!" Matt comes toward me and I clench my fists ready for him.

"You piece of shit!"

"Am I? I don't think so. You hit on women? Is that what gets you off?" I challenge him. Maybe I'm being a dick. Maybe I just need the release, but I egg him on until he moves. Just as he swings, I duck and counter it. Slamming my fist into his ribs, he stumbles back. I move in, hitting again and again until I hear Shane's mom. When did she move?

"Shane!" Her cries rip through the red fog that I've found myself in. Rushing up the steps, I follow the sounds of her screams when I see Shane. Shane's in the bathtub, blood dripping from her wrists. Her eyes are closed, and she looks peaceful.

"Move!" I roar rushing toward her. Everything inside of me breaks in this moment. I grab the towels and tie them tightly around Shane's wrists before lifting her in my arms. I drop onto my ass on the floor as her mom cries.

"Call an ambulance," I tell her. She moves but I don't. I reach for her neck, feeling for a pulse. It's there but it's not very strong. As I look down at her pale face, my stomach clenches.

"You can't do this to me, Shane. I might hate you but I fucking love you too. Don't you get it? How fucking torn I am? How can I let you go?" I shake my head as I stare at her closed eyes. This is wrong. This is right. I don't know what this is anymore. "Stay with me, Shane. Just… stay with me."

I can vaguely hear the sirens as they come closer. I wish I could call my brothers, but I can't. Not now. And Whisper? She will hate me. I caused this. I can't believe that she actually did this to herself.

"Shane, please." I beg the nothingness that lingers around us.

12

SHANE

I wake up with my hands restrained. It's not a surprise but the man sitting in the chair next to me is.

"What are you doing here?" His eyes slowly raise from his phone and lock with mine.

"Why wouldn't I be here?" Asshole.

"Leave, Steele. I don't want you here," I tell him.

"As if I give a shit what you want. What were you trying to do? Huh? Guilt trip my brother back into your life? He told me what you did." His words sting. I close my eyes and try to drown out the fact that he's sitting in my room. He doesn't understand, none of them do and I'll be damned if I tell any of them.

"Get out, Steele," I say, grinding my teeth together almost painfully.

"Not a chance in hell. Answer me," he growls.

"I don't owe you anything. I don't need to tell you anything." I hear the chair shift before a hand wraps around my throat. The machines go wild as he squeezes. My eyes pop open as I look up at the void in his eyes.

"All I have are my brothers. I won't let you rip him apart, Shane. He loved you once. It wasn't his fault he ran but you could have fought harder." Tears spring to my eyes as I try to reach for his hands but can't. I thrash around, trying to move when the door flies open. In seconds, Steele's hand is off my throat as he's slammed against the wall. Fists fly as I cry until security comes rushing in. The men rip Steele and Callan apart as Knox slowly strolls through the room as if nothing is happening.

"This is your fault," Knox says when he comes to stand next to my bed.

"Everything is. She's gone and that's my fault too." I cry harder. Knox looks down at me, his brows furrowed. He doesn't know. None of them do.

"Who?"

"Just leave."

"Who is she?" Knox asks once more, a little more edge in his tone.

"Please," I cry harder. The noise slowly settles around us when the room clears out. My eyes are clenched shut as I sob uncontrollably. So much that my chest aches. I've ruined many lives in my short time here on earth, I know that much but the everyday reminder is what really kills me. That's the thing that shreds what's left of my heart. I keep my eyes closed when the door opens. I don't care who it is this time. I don't really care what they do to me either. Steele should have finished what I started.

"You were very lucky, Shane." That's not a voice I recognize. Opening my eyes, there stands a young doctor glancing at the chart in his hands.

"If you say so." Now he looks up at me.

"You don't think so?" I shake my head. "Why is that?"

"Nothing good comes from me, Doc. When I'm around,

everyone hurts in some way," I admit. He nods and looks back at his clipboard as if it holds all the answers.

"We all feel that way at times. If your boyfriend hadn't showed up and attempted to stop the bleeding, I would be having a different conversation with your parents." I huff out a laugh. I'm pretty sure my mom doesn't really give two shits about what I did. She'd probably be happy if I never woke up and she didn't have to live with the secrets anymore.

"Parents? You mean the drunk and her husband?" I ask raising an eyebrow.

"We all handle things differently."

"How long?" I ask, tired of this conversation.

"How long what?"

"Until I can get out of here?"

"Right now. You're leaving now." Callan's voice thunders through the room as the door clicks shut behind him.

"I don't believe she is. Suicide attempts aren't to be taken lightly, Mr. Alder, as you very well know." What the hell did that mean? I turn my head and look from the doctor to Callan and back.

"And as you very well know, I don't give a shit what you think. She isn't going to be alone, Dr. Tazol." I'm so confused but I can feel the tension between the two of them. I would ask how Callan knows him, but I already know the answer to that. The Alder's run this town.

"Callan, I'd advise you against this," the doctor says once more as Callan moves toward me. He begins to undo the restraints from my arms and as soon as he does, I sit up and rub at my sore wrists.

"And again, I didn't ask you what you'd advise." The doctor moves toward Callan and that's when he snaps. He spins around, grabbing the man by the front of his shirt and slamming him against the wall.

"I'm sick of you meddling. That's all you do and all you're good for. If you want to keep practicing in Rolling Springs, I'd suggest you mind your own fucking business." The way Callan grits his teeth and snarls in the doctor's face makes me shiver. I've seen Callan angry. I've seen him pissed but this is something else. The man nods his head and Callan slowly releases him before turning and grabbing a bag I hadn't noticed he brought in. Tossing it at me, I catch it as I watch him.

"What's going on?"

"Put the clothes on." That's all he says, his tone rough as if he's ready to explode once again.

"Is this a good idea?" I ask. Now I feel like the doctor is right. I'm not so sure I should be leaving this hospital either, because frankly, I'm tired of life. Maybe I need to be here. Maybe I need the help or maybe I just need a break from my everyday life. Callan's chest rises and falls rapidly and when I don't move, he does. He grabs me around the waist, lifts me off the bed and stands me on my feet. His nostrils flare as I look into his eyes.

"I am sick of the questions." He steps closer, I step back. "I'm tired of the bullshit." Another step. "I told you to do something and now you are going to fucking do it, Shane." The last step and my back hits the wall.

"I wanted to die, Callan." The words slip out before I can rethink them. His eyes flash a little darker before he reaches up and runs his fingers across my throat. Just when I relax into his touch, he wraps them around and squeezes, much like his brother did. My eyes widen and my lips part as Callan cocks his head to the side and looks down at me menacingly.

"Yeah. I know that much. Why the hell do you think we're

here? But I can tell you this, Shane. You will never ever try that shit again. Do you hear me?" His teeth are grinding, his jaw tics. Something about the power and fury that radiates off him scares me. I've never been afraid of Callan before. "Answer. Me."

"Yes." The sole word comes out as a harsh whisper. Not that I could manage anything more if I wanted to.

"Now put the clothes on that are in that bag," he says nodding toward the bag on the bed. I nod my head rapidly as he releases me. Before he can take a step back, I mouth off again.

"This manhandling thing you and your brother keep doing is going to end." And just like that I'm pinned to the wall only this time not by my throat. It's his hard body pressed into mine. It's heat, it's cruel heat that slowly runs through my veins when I'm this close to him. It's the feel of him when it's only us. Why is he doing this to me? His hand comes up, gripping my chin between his thumb and forefinger, forcing my gaze to his.

"I've only just gotten started with you, Shane. As soon as you walk out that door, you belong to me. I. Will. Own. You." His words are a threat. One I'd like to challenge but I know better. Callan steps back and grabs the bag, throwing it at me once again. This time I catch it and pull the clothes out. He paces the floor as I slide the jeans and shirt on, pulling the hospital gown off and tossing it on the bed. Then I move to sit in the chair and slip my feet into the shoes he brought. All of mine I might add.

When I'm finally finished, I sit and watch him as he paces. His eyes are so distant, something dark lingering in them. He isn't here, in the moment, not really anyway. His mind is somewhere else.

"I'm ready, sir." The sir might have been too much but if he's going to play God and my boss, I'm going to make him work for submission if he ever gets it all. Callan slowly turns to look at me, a sparkle in his eyes.

"Sir? I think I like that."

"I don't care what you like. You've ruined everything!"

"Have I? What a goddamn shame that is isn't it, Shane? You wanted to die and now I'm going to make you wish you had." I cross my arms over my chest and glare at him. The stitches burn. Apparently I did a better job cutting than I thought I did if I needed to be stitched up.

"I'm not going with you."

"Oh, but you are. I told you, you belong to me now."

"I don't belong to anyone. I'm not an object you can play with, Callan!" I snap.

"But my heart is?" I didn't expect that. His eyes hold the question as it lingers between us. "My heart is a toy for you isn't it, Shane?" I shake my head unsure of what to say.

"You don't care about me, Cal. We all know what this is."

"Tell me then. What is this?"

"Pity." Dark laughter bursts from his mouth as he tips his head back.

"Pity?" he asks in amusement.

"Yes, it's pity."

"Pity for what? Because you tried to kill yourself? Or the fact that you've been beat by your stepdad? Come on, Shane! Have you met my family? My dad tried to have my brother beaten to death, and he doesn't even get my pity!"

"Then what is this, Callan?" I challenge him in return. He wants to play this game; I will play it with him.

"This is us."

13

——————

CALLAN

"Watch her. Do not let her out of your sight," I order Chance, one of my dad's men that has now become one of ours. He nods his head as I shove Shane in his general direction.

"I'm not going to be held hostage, Callan!" she screams. I smirk and look over at her.

"Did you forget the part where you tried to slice your wrists? You clearly can't be trusted alone," I remind her. I watch the redness creep across her face, her anger slowly coming to the surface.

"I didn't ask you to come save the day! Fuck you!"

"That will be later. Right now, I need to talk to my brothers. Play nicely with Chance. I hear he likes fighters," I add as I walk away. I know Chance wouldn't dare lay a finger on her. He knows that I'd rip his throat out if he did.

I stroll down the hall when I'm met with a fuming Whisper.

"You stole her?" she asks, hands on her hips, eyebrows in her hairline.

"Stole her?"

"Right from the hospital, Callan!"

"Is it really stealing when she belongs to me?" I question her. As much as I love Whisper, I won't fight her on this. Her arms fall to her sides as she thinks that over.

"Good point but damn. You just busted all in there and took her." I see the slight smile curling her lips.

"Something like that. Is Steele back?"

"Don't you dare dismiss me like that," she snarls.

"I'm not. I need to talk to Steele and you already know that she's here."

"And being held captive," she says.

"Is it really considered captive when—" She doesn't let me finish.

"When she's yours. Blah blah blah. I get it, Callan."

"Good. Don't go in there and give her false hope of getting out anytime soon, either," I tell her as I reach out and pull her into me. She wraps her arms around my waist as I press a kiss to the top of her head.

"Wouldn't dream of it. I consider myself the good one of the family." We both burst into laughter at her words.

"Then we're all pretty fucked." Whisper pushes up on her toes and kisses my cheek before sauntering off to her best friend's room. I keep going down the hall and round the corner into the office. Steele sits in the chair, his head in his hands.

"Bad day at the office?" I muse.

"Isn't that every day?" He looks up and I can see how tired he is. He's been working his ass off since the issue with our dad.

"What can I do?"

"Take the meeting on Thursday with the staff at Finstein's?" I shrug.

"What time?"

"Nine."

"Fine with me. I don't have class till four and then practice."

"You'll really take it?" He asks as if I was joking. I know most of the businesses my dad owned. I watched him when I was growing up, went to work on occasion with him.

"Of course. Finstein's isn't shit, Steele. I know most of them, anyway. They won't have any issues," I tell him. He nods his head and blows out a breath before leaning back in the old leather chair.

"How's Shane?"

"Stubborn." He snorts.

"That's new."

"She's... I don't know, different? Acting different."

"She tried to kill herself, Cal. Of course, she's different. Something is bothering her to the point she wanted to die, man." Leave it to Steele to be so comforting.

"What if I'm the reason?" Steele sits up straighter, his blue eyes darkening as he looks at me.

"Why did you try to kill yourself all those years ago?" My hand instinctively moves to my wrist. Steele's eyes follow my movements, a slight nod included.

"What are we doing about Carol?"

"What do you mean?"

"I mean, what the hell does she want? She didn't just show up to be our mother after over twenty years." He nods again.

"I know. We need to get back into the search and destroy state of mind Dad had us in. You remember looking into shit? We need to do that again. I know I've slacked off taking this on," he states.

"You haven't slacked off. You've been working your ass off to get shit in order. I need to help more."

"No, you need to take your ass to school so you can take this shit on when you graduate."

"Don't want this forever?" I tease sliding my hands into my pockets.

"Not a chance in hell. I don't mind working, Cal, I just don't want this full time." I nod my head in understanding. I already knew that.

"We got this, Steele. You know that right?"

"I know. Don't talk to me like some little bitch, brother." I laugh as he shoves out of his chair and moves toward me. When he's within arm's reach, he places his hand on my shoulder.

"I'm not really the fatherly type and shit," he says making me laugh. That's an understatement.

"You aren't a fatherly anything," Knox says walking into the room. "What is this? Kiss and hug day?"

"Fuck off," Steele hisses before turning his attention back to me. "I watched you struggle, Callan. I don't want to see you like that again. I can't." I nod remembering the day I brought the knife to my wrist and cut. I wasn't me. I wasn't who I was supposed to be and that hurt. I knew deep down that I didn't really want to die but I felt like it was my only option. The only way out of the misery my dad caused me.

"It won't happen again," I reassure him.

"What about her? You can't guarantee she won't try again," Knox chimes in.

"She won't. I got her. Don't worry." A slow smile crosses my face as Steele blows out a breath and shakes his head.

"You got your hands full with that one." Just as Knox finishes talking, I hear her scream. We all share a look before we take off running. I'm down the hall finding Whisper on the floor in tears she's laughing so hard. When I look up, Shane has a lamp in her hand and Chance is doubled over.

"What the hell is this?" Steele asks before I have the chance.

"Oh God. I can't breathe!" Whisper says laughing harder. "She…" More laughter. "She nutted him!" Her laughter gets louder and louder as I look between the three of them.

"With good reason," Shane adds, tossing the lamp on the floor by her feet.

"I didn't do anything!" Chance groans as he holds his junk.

"Someone please tell me what is happening?" I ask looking between the three once more. Whisper is still laughing on the floor, so I opt for the two that are semi with it.

"He grabbed me," Shane states crossing her arms over her chest. My eyes fly to Chance, fire burning in my gut.

"I did not! You are psycho," he hisses as he adjusts his shit once more.

"And you're ball-less," Shane says.

"Why did you hurt him?" I ask her. She turns to face me, raising an eyebrow.

"A better question is, why are you putting someone as weak as him in place to watch me? If I could kick him in the balls and watch him fall that easily, don't you think that's bad?"

"Jesus Christ. It's another Whisper," Knox groans. Whisper laughs as she climbs to her feet heading straight toward him.

"What the hell is wrong with another me?"

"So many things." Whisper punches his arm and shifts to move past me to get to Steele.

"Deal with your girl, Cal." With that, the three of them walk off followed by Chance. It's almost amusing to watch him trying to walk with his nuts in his throat.

"What are you going to do? Punish me? Send me to my room?"

"What did he do to you?"

"Nothing."

"Not him. Matt." At that, she gasps and steps back.

14

SHANE

I won't tell him. I don't care what he does to me, he isn't getting that part from me. I might have been stupid enough to trust him at one point but not anymore. I turn and walk back into my so-called room and try to slam the door shut, when he shoves it open.

"I wasn't finished," he growls.

"No, but I was."

"I will find out, Shane. You know that," he says with confidence. I have no doubt he will. He's an Alder for fuck's sake. He can find out anything he wants and when he digs deep enough, he will know the truth but not from my lips.

"Then go and find out," I tell him as I drop onto the bed. Callan runs his hand through his hair as he looks at me. Those bright blue eyes that used to sparkle all the time now hold sadness. I miss it—that sparkle.

"Why does everything with you have to be so damn hard?" I shrug trying to ignore him but just being this close to him does something to me. I can't explain it and I don't want to. I love the feeling too much to complain. It's almost like a sense of peace.

"Am I allowed to go to school, sir?" His jaw tics. The muscle jumps and I want to push his buttons even further. So, I do. I climb off the bed and move toward him, pressing my hand to his chest. I love how wildly his heart beats under my palm. It's the same way mine does when he's near me.

"What are you doing, Shane?" His tone is heavier, huskier now. Just how I want him.

"What do you want from me, Callan? You want me to be the good little obedient girl? You want me to submit to you?" I watch the way his lashes flutter slightly. His hand slowly comes up and his fingertips gently glide down my cheek.

"Do you have any idea what you do to me?"

"Do I make you hard, Callan?" I try to shift, lower my hand but he steps closer, pressing our bodies together tighter while he shakes his head.

"You don't get it do you?"

"Get what?" Something is shifting between us. There's something that feels like it's wrapping around my throat and strangling me.

"What you do to me. You make me insane, Shane. Everything about you drives me crazy." He licks his lips. "The things I'd do for you, have done. The things I know. God, Shane." He stares at me, his eyes so focused yet so confused. I don't understand this. I don't know what he's talking about and just as I'm about to ask, he grabs my hand in his and brings it to his wrist. Holding my finger, he slowly drags it down a jagged scar. I gasp as I look down and back at him.

"You—"

"There's so much about this life you don't know. So much about my dad that you never got to see. When I left you, it wasn't because I wanted to. And now, now I know what you did and my fucking heart is broken, Shane. This scar? It has *nothing* to do with you and yet *everything* to do with you. Don't you get that?" I open my mouth but what do I say? How do I respond to that? It doesn't matter because Callan doesn't give me the chance. He drops my hand and moves back toward the door.

"Stay with me," I whisper. His eyes shoot to mine but there's a war in them. One he isn't sure how to handle and to be honest, neither do I. I can't tell him what I've done or what I was made to do. I can't give him that piece of me and trust that he will still want me after that. So for now, this has to be enough.

"I'd give everything I have to stay with you, Shane. Everything, but you can't give me the truth that I need to hear from you." His eyes are sad as he turns and leaves the room. Something inside of me breaks, tears fall down my cheeks. He brought me here but I feel like I'm losing him. When I hear glass shattering I jolt, but I don't make a move to go and see. I know it's him. I could see the rage in his eyes, feel it radiating off his body. The door slowly opens and Whisper walks in.

"You okay?"

"What am I doing to him?" I ask her.

"This isn't your fault!"

"It is. It's all my fault! I ruined him, Whisper." She grabs my hand and tugs, dragging me from my room and down the hall. When we reach the living room, I see the shattered glass on the floor, Callan standing directly in the middle of it. Knox passes him a bottle of whiskey and I watch as he takes a long pull.

"Go get dressed," Steele says but my eyes remain on Callan. "I said go get dressed. We all need a break." Now I do drag my eyes to meet his and when he nods, I know he means me too.

"No," Whisper says loudly. "Not until this is fixed."

"What's fixed?" Knox asks crossing his arms over his large chest.

"This! Them! She can't blame herself for what's happening. I'm not having it."

"It is her fault," Knox says, causing me to cringe. I knew it was but just hearing him say it hurt.

"No, it's not!"

"She's right," Callan says softly. "It's not her fault, but I can fucking guarantee I will find out who and why." An involuntary shiver races through my body at his words. The darkness, the fury, the pain. Callan slowly drags his head around to look at me and nods. "You won't tell me. I'll find out."

"There's nothing to know, Cal."

"You want to be a little liar, Shane? Is that what you want?" God, his beautiful eyes are so dark, so distant.

"There's nothing to know."

"You and I both know that isn't true, now don't we? Go get dressed. We're going out."

"She just tried to off herself and you want to take her out?" Knox asks, looking between all of us. "Am I the only one that thinks it's a bad idea?"

"I'm fine." Gritting my teeth, I never break eye contact with Callan.

"She isn't going to act up tonight, are you, Shane?" Callan steps toward me, the sound of crunching glass beneath his feet. I want to shake my head, but I'm frozen in place by the air around us. When I don't answer him, his hand comes up to my chest before slowly moving higher. Wrapping his fingers around my throat, he tugs me toward him. "Isn't that right?"

"Yeah. I won't act up."

"Good girl. Now go change. Cover up what you did." The way his teeth grind tells me not to push him any further tonight.

Doing as I'm told, I spin around and walk back down the hall with Whisper oddly silent next to me when I hear Knox.

"Are we all going to pretend that having her around is a good idea? Like we don't have enough shit on our plates?"

"Did I ask you?" Callan roars loudly.

"I don't need to be asked! You're different, Cal. I don't know what that little bitch did to you but she messed you up, man. You're not you!" The scuffle that follows goes unheard as Whisper ushers me into the room.

"Callan isn't like Steele."

"Meaning?"

"Meaning, if you have a secret you better let it out. He doesn't like secrets, Shane." Her words fall softly, and I know she means them.

"Have you ever had something taken from you that you can never replace?" She looks up and finds my eyes, nodding. I nod along with her.

"That's your secret to keep," she whispers. She understands me. Whether we saw it at first or not, I think that's what drew me and Whisper together. Broken souls know each other. They gravitate to the other seeking solace that only another broken being could provide.

"Let's get sexy and drive them insane," she says wiping at a tear that slid down her cheek.

"I think I've done that enough. Besides, how am I going to cover these?" I ask raising my arms so she can see the bandages.

"Did you mean it? You didn't want to live?" Slowly lowering my arms, I sigh.

"Everything just got too heavy, Whisper. I honestly don't know what I want anymore."

"Well one thing I can say is, let's make them work for it tonight." I laugh as Whisper pulls the closet open and I'm a little shocked to see all the new clothes in it. She pulls out a long sleeve shirt that has the front and back cut out. I eye it as she does the same until she turns to me.

"This. Yeah, wear this!" Shoving it into my arms, she turns back and grabs some skinny jeans and boots.

"Do I want to know where this came from?"

"Did you really think Callan wasn't prepared to bring you here?" She laughs. I suppose she's right. The Alder boys don't do anything without thinking it over first.

"Are we sure I should go?"

"You've been practicing with me. We're going to show those two what we can do with these bodies tonight, girl." God, I love Whisper.

15

———

CALLAN

The club is packed. Maybe the guys were right. Maybe I needed to get out and have a good time. My head has been a complete mess for days. Maybe this is exactly where I need to be.

Whisper grabs Shane and drags her out into the middle just as Grimes Featuring i_o's song *Violence* comes on. I move through the crowd with my brothers right behind me ready to see what they have planned. It's nothing like I thought it would be. I knew Shane had been practicing with Whisper but damn.

"Fuck!" Knox yells above the crowd. I nearly elbow him in the chest, but I can't take my eyes off Shane. The two of them move slowly at first until the beat drops. Then they are all over each other. It's like a goddamn strip tease with their clothes on. Shane rolls her hips, popping them side to side before rocking them back into Whisper. My cock thickens in my jeans at the sight of her. Her eyes close, her arms move above her head as she arches her back and pops her ass out. I groan as I take in her frame, every goddamn curve of her body. Leddy heads our way, resting her hand on Knox's arm but he shrugs her off. I have no idea what is with those two and I don't really care. Shane is moving, her hands running over her body and I'm transfixed on her. Whisper spins around, pressing her ass into Shane's front and I sure as hell don't miss the groan from Steele. Hell, even Knox is adjusting his cock. Shane grabs Whisper's hip, rolling her own in time with her before pulling back and spinning around. She bends over, running her hands up her leg as I lick my lips. When I can't take anymore, I storm the dance floor listening to my brothers whistling as I go. Coming up behind her, I wrap my arms around Shane's waist and pull her back into me. She gasps as her head falls back onto my chest rolling to the side. I lean down and run my lips up the side of her neck as our bodies continue to move as one. That's when the music changes again. Shawn Mendes and Camila Cabello's *Senorita* comes on and I grab Shane's hand, spinning her away from me before pulling her in closely. She doesn't smile, just watches me as we both move. I press my body against hers, my hand tightly against her lower back. Up and down, in and out, we move. I keep her held tight as my body burns. Spinning her once more, I pull her back to my front.

"Callan." She says my name where only I can hear her. I let my lips roam her soft skin as sweat drips down my temples. In this moment, everything in life is perfect. Everything is as it should be but that can change at any time. Me and my brothers are prime examples of that. And even though I want to live in the moment and enjoy this time with Shane, something else is happening inside of me. I close my eyes just as the noise breaks through my thoughts. The floor shakes, the walls explode. Brick flies through the air, knocking us to the ground. I roll over and cover Shane with my body as screams ricochet through the club. People are running, others crying, some screaming.

"Steele? Knox!" I call out to my brothers. Glancing around, I don't see them. Panic takes over as I climb off Shane and drag her to her feet. With her hand wrapped up in mine, I move around the people, shoving my way past them.

"Steele?" I call out again.

"We're good!" I move toward the sound of his voice to find him, Whisper and Knox. I look between them, making sure everyone is good before I pull Shane into my chest. Holding her head against me, I keep my senses on high alert.

"What the hell was that?" Knox asks looking between us.

"Sounded like a bomb. Let's get the girls out of here," Steele says, grabbing Whisper.

"What about Leddy?" Whisper asks quickly. Darkness crosses Knox's features as he looks between all of us.

"I'll find her. Get them out," he says nodding toward Shane. Letting her out of my arms, we move toward the exit and out of the building. I can hear the sirens in the distance and just like when I found Shane, my heart beats a little faster. She must be able to feel it. She squeezes my hand tighter, and it's as if everything else just sort of fades for the moment.

"Unless we want to deal with the cops, we need to move," Steele says. I nod, agreeing that I don't want to deal with that shit tonight. Instead, we start walking toward the car when the first cop car rolls in. Instead of going toward the club, it pulls in, stopping right in front of us. Shit. That's never a good sign. We all watch as the asshole climbs out of his car but his gaze is on mine.

"Callan Alder," he says, making my skin crawl.

"Yeah."

"Put your hands behind your back." Shane gasps as I pull away from her. I step up to the cop and eye him.

"What's this about?"

"You're under arrest for the assault of Matt McCormick. Turn around." I do as I'm told with a smirk on my face.

"Assault?" Steele asks stepping closer.

"Yeah. I beat the shit out of him," I laugh. Knox snorts as he walks toward us now and Steele smiles.

"For her?" He nods over his shoulder. I nod back.

"Watch her."

"She isn't going anywhere," Whisper tells him with a smile of her own but it's Shane's eyes that bother me. When my gaze clashes with hers, there's something more in them. Her blues mesh with mine and I'm lost. The asshole jerks on the handcuffs, pulling me back but I never stop looking at her.

"I'll call the lawyer," Steele says pulling his phone out and dialing. The cop helps me into the car, slamming the door in my face before climbing back in the front. Once he closes the door, I start my own line of questioning.

"I already know this isn't about Matt. So, what is it?" That's not how we work. That's not how the Alder's work. We own the goddamn cops.

"Can't talk about it. You'll see when we get to the station." I don't know his name, but I know who he is. That fact alone should have him opening his mouth, but he doesn't. So instead of pushing him, I sit quietly as we ride through Rolling Springs until we pull up at the station. He pulls around back before climbing out of the car and letting me out. I watch him as he nods at the door. As soon as I'm inside, he grabs the cuffs and takes them off me. I turn with my hands clenched ready for a fight.

"Don't hit my officer." Glancing over my shoulder, I smirk at Blake. Once his dad was dead, he asked about becoming the sheriff. Wasn't that a sweet deal for him? No longer the mayor but the asshole was still on our payroll.

"Why not?"

"Want more charges?"

"As if I had any to begin with." He motions for me to follow him and I spin around and do so. He ushers me into an office where I drop into the first chair I can find.

"There are so many things we need to discuss."

"Like why I was arrested to begin with. Did that asshole really press charges?" Blake looks amused as he walks around and takes his seat behind his new desk.

"Yeah, he came in. You broke his nose," he says as I shrug.

"Lucky that's all he got."

"We aren't here about him, Callan."

"Then spit it out, Blake. Why am I the only one here?" It doesn't make sense considering everyone knows that Steele has been handling the family and all its affairs. So why isn't he here?

"That's the thing. We had to make it look like we were bringing you in on charges."

"Do I get the little jumpsuit too?" I ask sarcastically.

"There's someone in town. We don't know what she wants," he adds.

"Who?" Leaning forward, I rest my elbows on my knees as I watch him for an answer.

"Carol Alder. Has she been by?"

"More than once. What the hell does she have to do with anything?"

"Do you know why your mom left, Callan?" I shrug and lean back in the chair, my legs spread wide as I relax.

"She said Dad made her. Threatened her." A smile tugs across Blake's face that pisses me off a little.

"That's not the story I was given."

"Stop playing games, Blake, and spit it out! What the hell do you want to tell me?" I'm sick of him already. I didn't like the idea of the little bastard being the sheriff but at the same time we didn't want him running off someplace else and opening his mouth about our town either. So, like the good gentlemen we are, we compromised with the little shit.

"From what my father told me, she left on her own. She wanted the business and couldn't get it. She wanted the family, but she knew she had no pull to have it all. They think she went to find someone that could help her."

"Help her what? No one else has any rights to the family but us." He shakes his head.

"I don't know the answer here, Callan. I just know that she's back and now we have bombs going off in a club that you and your brothers just happen to be at. Something isn't adding up." Now that he says it, I see it. Could he be right?

"She kills us, no one left to fight her," I mumble as it all starts making sense. But why? Why does she need it all? Steele was already talking about cutting her in on one of the businesses. Hell, that alone would make her a millionaire. Why go to all the trouble of killing her own sons?

"I see you thinking, and I don't have any answers. This was all I got," Blake speaks.

"And Matt?"

"What about him?"

"Is he taken care of?" I ask.

"He's been warned. He won't be a problem but where is Shane?"

"What do you care?" I see his eyes, the way they lit up when he said her name. What the fuck? Does he have a thing for her? I'm out of my seat and around the desk grabbing him by the neck.

"She's mine, Blake. You got me?" He nods, his face turning a shade of red that makes me hard. I shouldn't like it so much but damn.

"Yeah, got it." I release him and storm toward the door, pissed that I had to be brought in here. Pissed that my mom is doing this. Pissed that I still hold Shane's secret inside of me.

16

SHANE

"Hey, McCormick. If you pace anymore, I might actually think you care about my brother," Steele says from his spot in the chair. I flip him off and keep walking, my arms crossed over my chest. It's been an hour since the police picked him up. It's only been a few minutes since the lawyer left here and headed that way.

The door flies open and we all move to look. Callan walks in, sweat dripping from his temples as he tries to catch his breath.

"What the hell happened?" Steele moves to ask first.

"It was a set up. All that club shit was a set up. Guess who they think did it?" he says looking at his brother, a slow grin tugging across his face.

"Us?"

"Not this time, brother. Mom."

"Mom?" Knox chimes in.

"Yeah. Thinks she's after the family name and all that comes with it. Blake gave me one hell of a story. He said Dad didn't want her and she wanted everything. She took off to figure out how to get it."

"And that took twenty years?" I find myself asking.

"Apparently." His growl wasn't at my question. If I thought I had a fucked-up family, this one takes the cake. The Alder family is notorious around here for being a well-oiled machine, but they are by far, the most fucked-up family I've ever met.

"So, we feel her out. Play her game." Steele shrugs like it's no big deal.

"Play her game? How?" Knox asks lighting up a joint.

"Get inside her head. Let her think we're on her side. Hand her a few gifts along the way. She isn't as smart as she thinks she is if she showed up here," Callan states in a matter of fact tone. The guys all look at each other briefly before they nod. Steele yawns, moving to stand and grabbing Whisper as he goes.

"I'm going to bed. This night turned to shit really quick."

"Yeah. Me too. I have that meeting tomorrow with Finsteins." Steele nods at Callan before dragging Whisper down the hall. I wrap my arms around myself and turn, following behind them. I'm not sure what I was expecting. Callan to follow me? I know he still harbors some deep resentment toward me and I don't know how to fix that. Walking into the room they had set up for me, I fall onto the bed and sigh loudly.

"Rough night." I close my eyes and pretend to not hear him, not wanting to fight or argue. I'm still shaken up after what happened at the club. I don't move until I feel the bed shift. Turning my head to the side, I see Callan lying on his back, his arm thrown over his eyes.

"Were you hurt?" I ask, wondering.

"No. You?"

"Not really." He turns his head, his eyes coming to meet mine. In this moment, the air is sucked from the room. I feel like

I'm suffocating and there's no way to drag a breath into my lungs. Callan rolls onto his side, his hand coming up to my cheek as he watches me.

"Not really?" he asks, arching his eyebrow.

"I'm just a little shaken up is all." He nods as his eyes burn into me. This is what I've missed the most about him. The heat, the way he used to look at me. So when he scoots closer, I don't protest.

"It was scary." His words are soft just like his lips when they touch mine. My heart leaps into my throat as he slowly moves his mouth over mine. Each stroke of his tongue against my lips becomes more demanding until I let him in. The growl that leaves him runs straight to my core.

Callan moves to roll on top of me and I gladly spread my legs for him. He makes himself comfortable as he grinds himself against me. Heat coils in my stomach, my hands finding their way into his hair. Each tug earns me a growl, so I don't stop. Heat pools between my thighs and I don't know if it was a good thing I changed when I got home or not. Callan drags his hand down my side and in between us. I whimper against his lips when his finger slips under my shorts and straight where I want them.

"Shane?" He says my name like it's the last thing he may ever say and I can't say that I don't like hearing it in that husky tone of his. When I don't answer, he slips his finger inside of me and slowly begins to massage me. A breath leaves my lips so lightly that I feel like I'm floating. He slowly adds another finger and I find myself arching into his touch.

"Tonight at the club, I have never found you as sexy as I did when you were dancing with me." My eyes slowly open and lock with his. I know the guys all love to dance. It's just in their nature but I was never that good at it until Whisper came along. I would try but I would basically look like one of those blow up guys that flip all around in front of a car wash.

"Really?" I ask as his fingers keep moving inside of me. I gasp when he changes their position.

"Sweat dripping off you. Your body pressed against mine. The way you looked at me. Fuck, Shane," he curses under a husky breath. His fingers slip out of me and he jerks my shorts down my legs. I watch him as he reaches up and pulls his shirt over his head and tosses it to the side. The muscles, the tattoos, the sweat that still clings to his skin all beg for me to touch them. He finishes stripping out of his clothes before motioning for me to sit up. I do and he rips my shirt over my head and unclasps my bra. His warm fingers dance over my flesh as he slips the straps down my arms. Before I can think or react, he grabs me, flipping us both so that I'm on top of him. He runs his hands up my stomach, grabbing my breasts in each hand and massaging them. My body begins to move on its own, rubbing against him.

"Cal," I moan as he plucks at my nipples. He runs his hands back down, stopping at my stomach and my heart lurches into my throat.

"I'm keeping you, Shane." It's a statement, one I'm not sure I'm ready for just yet. There's so much tension and too many secrets between us for him to say that to me. It doesn't matter to him, not when he flips me so I'm on my back and his hard cock is pressing into me. I don't try to stop him and I know I should. Closing my eyes, I feel the tip barely press into me before his hands are on my face.

"Look at me, Shane." I shake my head but when his lips touch mine once more, I do it. I open my eyes and they lock with the bluest sky colored eyes that have forever held my heart.

"I'm not like you," I whisper.

"That's why I want you, Shane. I don't want someone like

me. I want someone that completes me." Tears burn the back of my eyes, but I don't let them fall.

"I can't tell you what you want to know, not yet." He nods and rests his forehead against mine as he thrusts the rest of the way into me. I gasp, my hands coming to cling to his shoulders.

"I know."

"And you will hate me when I tell you," I remind him.

"I know that part too," he whispers before licking the lone tear that slid down my cheek. Callan pushes up, grabbing my leg and throwing it around his hip as he begins to thrust. Each one is heaven. Each one is hell and he can feel it too. He might be keeping me but somewhere deep down he still hates me for what he's learned, and in the back of my mind I know exactly what it is. I just can't bring myself to say it to him. Not yet.

"Fuck, Shane," he growls before picking up his pace. I slide my hands over his shoulders, down his chest and feel all the muscles move as he moves. Each one is perfect. Perfected from his years of playing football and being who he is. Sweat coats my palms as I run them back up and around his neck, pulling his lips to mine.

"Fuck me, Callan." That's all he needed to hear. His lips crash onto mine, his hips bucking and taking control. And just like we were made for each other, I ride the high that only Callan can give me.

I adjust my suit jacket as I stand in front of the table looking at the head of Finstein's, one of our companies we inherited from our dad. Finstein's specializes in computer software that we make good use of when we need to find things.

"We're all very sorry to hear about your father, Callan," Greg, the man in charge says. I nod once, trying to be respectful when in reality they all know we killed that bastard. They all saw it coming.

"Thank you. I appreciate that but let's stay on topic, shall we? You know I'm here because my brothers and I have taken power over all the companies. As of right now, Steele is handling things while Knox and I finish our degrees."

"When you do finish, will one you of you be taking over?" I turn my attention to the woman on my right.

"That hasn't been discussed but more than likely, yes. The reason for the meeting today is to make sure that everyone is on board with us being in charge now. As far as internal affairs here, nothing changes. The only difference is now you answer to us instead of our father. Is that going to be an issue for any of you?" I glance around the table not seeing anyone that wants to fight me on this. That's always a good sign. "I also know that my father was a greedy man. His pay grade was bullshit to be honest and that is going to change in the near future. We have appointments with the accountants coming up in a few months' time and after that I can assure you, a raise will be in order for all of you." Of course no one is going to complain about more money.

"Will you be coming into the office more?" Cheryl asks from her spot. My eyes slowly find hers and I watch as she licks her ruby red painted lips. Yeah, I fucked her before but that doesn't mean I'm going back for a repeat. Cheryl is younger, not as young as us but she doesn't fit your typical suit and tie pencil pushers either. She's beautiful with long blonde hair that she keeps tied up in a tight bun. I remember running my fingers through that hair once upon a time.

"Not me. Perhaps Knox will be in the future. For now, we plan to keep things flowing as smoothly as possible with meetings as we see fit. Of course, if you ever have any problems don't hesitate to reach out, you should all have our numbers now. Before we go, I want to mention Carol Alder. She is not to be involved in any way, shape or form. Nothing is to be discussed with her or in her presence. I know a few of you are aware of who she is; the others don't need to be. She means nothing to this company. Is there anything else you want to discuss while I'm here?" I ask, glancing around the table once more. Everyone seems to be happy with the change so I nod.

"Good. Then this meeting is over. Thank you all for your understanding and patience while we work out the kinks." Everyone stands and grabs their things, turning to leave, everyone but her. I should have known Cheryl would stick around and see how far she can push me but the fact is, she isn't going to get far. I grab my bag and heft it over my shoulder knowing I need to be in class soon for a test and standing here reminiscing on the past with Cheryl will hinder that.

"Why aren't you coming around?" she asks, stepping up in front of me, her palm resting on my chest.

"I'm not needed."

"I don't think that's true," she purrs, undoing a few buttons on my dress shirt. I clear my throat and take a deep breath through my nose.

"Did you think I came here just for you?" Her eyes shoot to mine.

"I heard about Shane. Are you back with her?"

"Are you really going to stoop so low that you can't keep your hands off a college boy, Cheryl?"

"You are no boy, Callan. We all know just how much of a man you are." One of her hands moves to grab my cock, giving it a rough squeeze. I groan, pressing it into her hand a little harder.

"Well this man, as you say, isn't interested in you anymore." I reach up and grab her wrist, twisting it painfully until she flinches and steps back. Releasing the grip on her, I walk past and out of the conference room waving at a few people as I go. Once I'm in the elevator, I loosen the tie from around my neck. I never understood the appeal of this shit. My dad always wore a suit and tie but the three of us? We can't stand them. Once the elevator reaches the first floor, I climb out and walk hurriedly to my car and jump in. I start it up and then call Steele.

"How did it go?"

"Good. Everyone's on board just like I thought they would be. No one has an issue except Cheryl." He chuckles.

"And what's her issue?"

"She won't be riding my cock," I tell him. I weave through

traffic as I give him the breakdown of the overall meeting and how it went smoothly.

"You heading to class?"

"Yeah. Just pulling in."

"Check on Whisper. She was being a bitch when she left here," he says, sounding a little off himself.

"Something I need to know?"

"No. Just that she was being a bitch is all." I laugh this time because I know exactly how Whisper gets.

"I'll take care of her. I'll give her nipples a few good sucks, have her come all over my fingers then she should be fine." I hear him growl and just as he's about to say something, I click the phone off. Smiling to myself, I love getting under his skin. Whisper wasn't the first girl that we shared a taste of but I can honestly say she was the last. If anyone even looks at Shane like they want a piece of her, I have a bad feeling I'm going to lose my shit. I let it slide the other day because I wanted to prove a point but now she's mine and only mine.

With my bag over my shoulder, I hurry to class. As soon as I step inside, Whisper spots me and snorts a laugh as I make my way toward her.

"What the fuck are you wearing?"

"What? I can't pull off the suit?" I ask dropping my bag on the floor and modeling for her. Whisper laughs and doesn't seem to be in a bitchy mood like Steele had said. She seems happy enough to me.

"I don't think there's anything the three of you can't pull off. You all ooze that damn sex appeal and it doesn't matter if you wear a suit, jeans, or a trash bag," she huffs. There she is. I slide into the seat next to her, wrap my hand around the back of her neck and pull her face to mine. I'm so close I can feel her breath dance over my lips.

"Whatever your problem is, say it now."

"Or what?" she challenges me back.

"Or I will take you out of this class and finger fuck you until you can't walk straight. Then I'll call Steele and tell him exactly how much you liked it," I warn her. Whisper watches me for a second before blowing out a breath knowing my threat is real.

"He won't use condoms." What the hell? That's what she's worried about? I drop my hand and lean back in my seat as if she never spoke. "Did you hear me?"

"I heard you."

"You don't think that's an issue?" she asks, her anger clear as day now.

"Not really. We don't like condoms, Whisper."

"I don't like kids, Callan. See the problem?" she hisses. I shake my head and cross my arms over my chest before glaring at her.

"Did you think my brother wouldn't want kids at some point in his life?"

"Did he ask me if I wanted kids?" she smarts off right back. This. This right here is why I love her little defiant ass.

"Does it matter?" I question her, raising my eyebrow. I can see that fire building inside her and I almost laugh.

"Yes, it fucking matters! I don't want my kid to end up like me!" Whisper slides out of her chair and grabs her bag heading for the door.

"Whisper!" Shit. Now I need to fix this. I grab my shit and follow her only to find her in the hall in Shane's arms. Shane's eyes meet mine, a sadness in them.

"Whisper? I'm sorry. I hate to be the one to break this to you but you aren't like them. Even if you have a baby, you would never abandon it." Shane flinches, Whisper turns to face me, and I feel like a complete asshole.

"No, I wouldn't but that doesn't mean I want one, Cal. This is all too new, too much." I nod my head and open my arms. Whisper falls right into me, wrapping her arms around my waist as I hold her.

"I should go," Shane says softly. With one hand, I reach out and grab her, keeping her from leaving. Whisper pulls back, smirking up at me.

"Let me guess, you didn't use them either, did you?"

"None of your business."

"What is it with you guys? You want like millions of little Alder's running wild?" Whisper asks with a smile on her now happy face.

"Maybe not millions." I shrug.

"I need to go," Shane says, a hitch in her voice. I ignore her.

"Hundreds? You guys are so young," Whisper whines. It's cute seeing her flustered like she is.

"So? Gives us extra time to make more right?" She rolls her eyes and presses a kiss to my cheek before turning and walking away. Once she's out of sight, I drag Shane in front of me.

"Going somewhere?" I ask.

"I have to get ready for the game tonight. I'm covering for Sam," she says but she doesn't sound like herself. Something is bothering her, and I know exactly what it is. I'm pushing her.

"What's wrong?"

"Nothing."

"Don't lie, Shane. I don't like it when people lie to me." The growl has her flinching.

"It's nothing. Why are you in a suit, anyway?" Okay. I'll let her change the subject if that's what she wants but only for now. Eventually, I will get the truth out of her.

"I had a meeting I told Steele I'd handle this morning before class but seeing how now I am missing said class, I need to find something else to do. Or someone." I let my eyes fall to her lips as she slowly begins to smile. Damn, I've missed that smile for so long.

"There's always the locker room," she teases, pressing her body into mine. I wrap my arm around her back, keeping her pressed against me when I hear it. Releasing Shane, I turn to see her, Carol Alder, my so-called mother walking down the hall. Her tall stiletto shoes clicking over the marble floors as she walks toward us.

"Ma'am! You can't be here."

"I need to speak with my son!" We lock eyes as she storms down the hall.

"What the hell is she doing?" Shane mumbles next to me.

"No idea."

"Oh, you're here," Carol says, eyeing Shane in disgust.

"I do go to school here," Shane smarts off.

"And she's mine," I growl, pulling her into my side. Is it wrong that I want to smirk in Carol's face?

"We need to talk," she says looking directly to me.

"No, we don't. I think I've heard enough. You said your piece at the house the other night and Steele is making his decision."

"It's not that easy, Callan."

"Isn't it? You came back. I don't understand why or what you want but here you are. You can't just show up at the school and demand to see me. I am here to learn, to get my degree." Jesus, I sound like my dad. Almost to the point it makes my skin crawl.

"I heard you were in that… that club when it exploded." I take a calming breath so that I don't do something stupid that I might regret later.

"We were. All of us," I say as calmly as I can. Carol moves, pulling me into a hug as she fake sobs on my shoulder.

"I'm so glad no one was hurt. That could have been devastating." I roll my eyes. I can't help it. She's lost her damn mind coming here and acting like this for show.

"Are you?" I hiss. She pulls back and looks me in the eye, a lie on the tip of her tongue.

"Of course, I am. You're my son." I feel the bile rise in the back of my throat before I take a step away from her. Shaking my head, I turn and pull Shane with me when she speaks once more.

"How is your mother and is it your stepfather, Shane? It's been ages since I've seen them." Fire erupts inside of me and I know that was a jab at Shane. Before I can rethink it, I'm spinning around and moving toward her. I grab Carol around the throat, slamming her against the nearest door. The students inside scream a little from the impact but no one makes a move to stop me.

"I don't know what your game is or what you think you're going to achieve by coming back here but if you ever speak to her, look at her, or just breathe in her general direction, I will snap your neck. Do you understand me? *Mom.*" That last bit came out harsher than I wanted it too but by the way her eyes widen, she gets the picture.

"Did you know?"

"Know what?"

"About her and her stepfather," she says, pissing me off further. Shane gasps behind us, a small sob escaping her as she does. I don't need to turn and look, I hear her feet hitting the marble as she takes off running.

"What's your play here, Carol? You want it all? You want a piece? What is it?"

"Everything. I want everything I deserve and I will bring this whole town down around me to get it," she snarls. So much for us playing her games, now she's going to play ours.

"Is that so?" I ask, cocking my head to the side to study her face. I bet she was even more beautiful once. Maybe before the hate and anger overtook her.

"Your father ruined me. He took everything I had and left me with nothing."

"From what I hear you didn't have a very hard time saying goodbye to your kids when you left." She watches me, a small smirk playing across her face.

"You were always the pawns, Callan. Don't you see that? Your father wanted boys. He wanted men that he could groom to take over the company. Do you know why there are only three of you?" I grit my teeth not sure that I want to hear what's about to come out of her mouth. "The first one was a girl."

What? We have a sister? A sister older than Steele? No. I've never met her. I don't know anything about a sister. My hand slowly releases, and Carol instantly reaches up and rubs her throat.

"I see you didn't know that part."

"Who is she?" Carol shrugs.

"She's no one. She's dead," she says like it's no big deal to her. None of this makes sense.

"What do you mean? How?"

"Think about it, Callan. Your father only wanted boys. The way he treated you three, the way he made you who you are. You're a smart man, put the pieces together." With that she turns and walks off the way she came leaving me stunned into silence. He killed her, or had her killed. If we did really have a sister and Dad didn't want her, he wouldn't keep her around. He would get rid of her. My God, what kind of sick fuck was he?

18

SHANE

I couldn't stand there and listen to her. I couldn't see him doing that to her and knowing what I know. So, I did what I do best and ran. Now I'm sitting in the stands with Whisper, watching the game. Callan had practice right after school and then again right before the game started. This is one of their hardest teams to play against and the new coach wanted to make sure they were all ready.

"You okay?" Whisper asks leaning into me. I nod but I don't look over at her. That's when I feel her arm go around me. Steele is hollering and screaming next to her as we watch the game.

"Run, Cal! Fuck, I should have stayed on the team," he grumbles. "Look at them! Like a bunch of pussies." Whisper and I share a glance before we both start laughing. God, I needed that.

"What?" Steele asks, looking between us.

"Nothing. Carry on," Whisper says with a huge smile on her face.

I watch Knox pass Callan the ball before he takes off down

the field. Everyone is on their feet cheering him on including me. I don't know why I get so excited watching him play. Maybe it's because that's the only time he can truly be a college football player and not a man that his Dad forced him to be. The crowd roars as Callan runs back with his finger held in the air. He got the touchdown. Not like that surprises anyone. The Alder boys all know how to play football.

"I'm going to grab a water. Want anything?" I ask, looking between Whisper and Steele.

"Yeah, a water," Steele says. I nod and jog down the bleachers and around the back toward the concession stand. Just as I pass the bathrooms, someone grabs me and pulls me inside. I'm about to open my mouth and scream when a hand comes down to stop me. What the hell?

"You are a thorn in my side, Shane." Carol? What the hell is she doing now? She walks around to stand in front of me while someone keeps me held in place. "You are warping him. All of this could have been so easy if you wouldn't have come back. I thought that Matt would have killed you by now but clearly that idiot can't do anything right." Carol nods and the hand slowly leaves my mouth.

"What are you doing, Carol?" I ask through gritted teeth.

"You had a child, yes?" Blood whooshes in my ears. How does she know that? "Don't bother asking a stupid question. I won't tell you how I know anything, not when you're screwing my son."

"What do you want?"

"I want what I'm owed. I want what was rightfully mine before that man stole it all!"

"I won't help you, Carol. If that's what you think, you're insane." She smiles and presses her pretty manicured nail into my cheek. I wince at the pain but that isn't the worst thing I've ever felt.

"You will if you want that little girl to live."

"What are you talking about? She's been adopted. She is living."

"You wanted to keep her, didn't you?" She steps back, lowering her hand. "You wanted to keep that little love child."

"He raped me. That doesn't count as love in my book." I can hear the screams of the crowd, the announcer's voices over the speakers.

"But you wanted that child. You wanted something that would love you the way your mother didn't love you. Something that was yours and only yours." God, she's disgusting.

"Go to hell!" I roar. Her hand flies across my cheek, her nail ripping through my skin. I can feel the blood as it blooms on my flesh.

"I've been there my whole life, Shane. Hell, that is. All I wanted was what was mine and they took it! I had a little girl once too. Did you know that?" she asks, looking distant.

"What?"

"I had a daughter. She was beautiful. All eight pounds of her. He took her away from me because she wasn't a boy. Boys were all he needed. A girl was a complication that he didn't want. I begged him, pleaded with him to just let me keep her and I'd give him more boys than he could ever ask for," she says, a sob catching in her throat.

"Oh my God," I whisper.

"He didn't agree. She was taken from me in the most brutal of ways, Shane. Where your daughter went into the foster system, mine went into the cold dark dirt beneath our feet." My mouth parts but no words will form. What do I say to that? I knew their dad was by far one of the worst people I'd ever met in my life but to kill a child? A baby at that? It shouldn't surprise me the way it does since I knew how the boys were treated when I first met them, but it does.

"Is it all making sense to you now?" I shake my head because I honestly don't understand what she wants from me.

"That little girl of yours… looks so much like your real father. Isn't it amazing how that works? Genetics and all?"

"What?" I fight the hold the man has on me, but it does no good. "How would you know what she looks like? What did you do?"

"Nothing yet. That's where you come in. You are all nice and cozy with the boys once again. I want information. I want names. I want every place they frequent and what times and days. I want to know every fucking step they take." I shake my head. No way in hell will I cross Callan like that. I just got him back. I can't lose him again. I won't. The more I shake my head the angrier she becomes. She holds her hand out to the man holding me. He moves one arm quickly, passing her a small knife before grabbing my head and holding it still. Carol steps closer, her eyes wild with darkness as she presses the tip into my flesh.

"You will do it. You will do everything I want or I will kill that little girl. I will slit her throat just like that bastard did to mine," she hisses as she drags the blade down my cheek. I cry out in pain as the blade tears through my flesh. Pain shoots through me but just as I'm about to say something more, the man releases me, letting me fall into a crumbled mess on the floor. I reach up and cover the cut as I cry and look at the floor. Her shoes come into view and the thought of slitting her throat crosses my mind, but clearly Callan and the guys underestimated her. She has people—or at least one. Her pointed toe slams into my ribs before I hear her turn and walk away. A guttural scream rips from my lungs as I lay on the floor a bleeding mess. I can hear the screams; I can hear the announcer saying the game is over. We won.

The door opens and a woman screams as I lift my head and look up. Her eyes lock with mine, horror all over her face. I'm sure I look a mess.

"Are you okay? Oh, my God." I shake my head before laying it back on the floor crying until I can't breathe.

"In there!" someone yells outside the door. Then the door is being kicked open and dark dirty boots step in front of me.

"Shit," Steele hisses as he leans down and lifts me in his arms. Still crying, I let my head fall onto his chest and cry harder. Would she do it? Would she really hurt that little girl if I don't do what she wants? How am I going to tell them that? How can I tell them that Matt raped me and I got pregnant all those years ago?

Steele carries me out of the bathroom and I faintly hear Whisper's voice as my head becomes full of thoughts.

"Go get Callan and Knox!"

"No. They just won," I tell him when the words finally come out.

"I don't give a shit. You're hurt and Callan will lose his shit if he doesn't know." Steele's voice is as hard as ever as I'm carried from the stadium. My heart hurts. My face hurts. But most of all, I'm angry. I'm afraid. What if Callan hates me once he finds out? What if they all turn against me once they know that I had to give her up?

"Where is she?" I hear Callan growl as we make it into the parking lot.

"I got her," Steele says, the words rumbling in his throat. I can feel movement around me, but I keep my eyes clenched shut.

"Jesus. Whoever did this to you, I'm going to kill them. Nice and fucking slow too." Callan's words make me cry harder. He can't kill his own mom. I wouldn't let him do it. Callan slips his arms under me, taking me from his brother before climbing into the back of the SUV. He holds me in his lap as everyone climbs in. He isn't in his uniform so I assume he changed quickly. Not that I bother to open my eyes and look. I don't. I keep them closed, praying this is all a bad dream. That I will wake up and none of this really happened and as I cry harder and inhale the scent of Callan, I wish I was never born.

19

CALLAN

My knee bounces up and down as we sit in the waiting room. I damn near knocked the doctor out when he told me to leave the room. We own this town! I shouldn't have walked out the way I did but she looked like she needed space.

"Calm down," Knox growls next to me.

"Fuck you."

"That's enough. Both of you stop," Steele states in a hardened tone. Whisper chews her fingernail in the corner not looking at anyone. I'm on the verge of exploding. I want answers. I want to know who hurt her and why. There are so many questions that are unanswered right now and that pisses me off further. I glance up when I see a wheelchair coming our way with Shane sitting in it. She won't look up, just stares at the floor. I leap to my feet and rush toward her, dropping to my knees. My hand comes up to her cheek before pulling back when I see the stitches. They cut her deep enough that she needed stitches!

"Shane?" I say her name softly but when she doesn't respond, I look to the doctor.

"She has eight stitches. She will need to take these antibiotics to ensure she doesn't get an infection. Otherwise, she will heal up fine. There will be a scar but over time that will fade. The bruising on her ribs will fade. She's ready to go. She needs lots of rest and if anything changes, bring her back." I nod as Knox moves in behind the wheelchair to push her out. My heart is hammering in my chest, rage simmering in my veins. As much as I want to hate her, I know that I don't. She's always had a piece of my heart and whether I want to admit that or not, it's true.

We all walk outside, and Steele and Whisper move to get the car. I glance at Knox and he takes the hint, following behind them.

"You know I won't let them get away with this," I tell her. She looks up at me, something dark in her eyes.

"You have no choice."

"What the hell does that mean? You think that I'm not going to kill whoever did this to you?" She huffs out a breath and shakes her head.

"I'll explain it all later."

"Now, Shane! Explain it now!" I roar. The car pulls up and Whisper jumps out shoving me back a step.

"She's hurt, asshole." I step toward her and she raises an eyebrow to challenge me. I know better than to hit her, or lay a fucking finger on any woman. That isn't me. So I step back and watch as she helps Shane stand, noting the wince as she grabs at her ribs. How does she expect me to not make someone pay for this? For what they did to her? Without thinking about it further, I close the door as Whisper climbs in the back with Shane and Steele while Knox and I get in the front seat. I don't look back the whole silent ride back to the house. Even when the car comes to a stop and they all climb out, I stay rooted in place.

"You want to talk about it?" Knox asks after he opens my door and stands there, hands resting on the roof.

"She said I have no choice but to let this go." He snorts a laugh.

"Yeah, she can think that all she wants."

"That's what I was thinking too but she was serious, Knox. Whoever did this, I don't know what they said to her. What they threatened her with," I tell him. He sighs and stands back allowing me to get out of the SUV. Then he follows me inside where the rest of them are sitting in the living room. My eyes move to each of them, resting on hers.

"Matt has always hated me. It wasn't a big a secret to anyone that knew us. I was a pawn in my mom's sick game of life. I was the good girl that kept her mouth shut so that the money kept coming in. I hated it. Hated them. Mostly him at the time," she says before clearing her throat. I note the wince once more as the growl works its way up my throat.

"You don't have to do this," Whisper states. Steele snorts a laugh.

"Like hell she doesn't."

"She's hurt, Steele!"

"Yeah? And my brother is about thirty seconds away from murder! She needs to tell us what the fuck is going on before he ends up in prison!" Steele isn't joking around now. He can see it, feel the murderous intent as it radiates off me.

"I need to say it! Just… give me a second." Knox moves to grab a bottle of water, handing it to Shane. We all watch her take a long pull before settling herself once more.

"He raped me."

"That son of a bitch!" I don't wait to hear more. I turn and slam my hand into the wall. Pain bursts brightly through my hand as my head falls forward.

"My mom knew about it. It was too late when I found out," she says. That catches my attention. I turn to face her, my hand throbbing.

"What? Found out what?" Shane looks around the room at everyone before focusing on Whisper. It kills me that she can't look to me for help. That she can't look at me for the comfort that she needs right now.

"That I was pregnant." A silence fills the room as we all let that sink in. I knew. I knew that part, that's the part that I wanted her to tell me because from everything I saw, it looked like they were together. Like she was fucking him because she wanted to. I put her through hell for nothing. Nothing! Regret isn't something I'm used to feeling but there it is right in the pit of my damn stomach like a lead weight. Acid burns the back of my throat as I think about the way I treated her. She didn't deserve it. None of it. Fuck!

"What happened tonight?" Steele asks, keeping his tone the same.

"Your mom pulled me into the bathroom. She had some guy hold me. Said that I was supposed to get information from you guys and turn it over to her," she tells us.

"And are you?" Steele asks. That's it. I turn and lunge for him, but Knox is already there pulling me back.

"What the fuck kind of question is that, Steele?"

"A good one! Shane hasn't been around, Callan. Dad made sure of that and now we learn this shit?"

"I didn't ask for *this* shit. You can all go to hell!" Shane explodes, shoving herself off the couch when Steele is on her. He shoves her back down and she flinches from his touch. Fury rises inside of me, but I know he's just trying to calm the situation.

"We aren't done here."

"What else do you want? All the gory details of what he would do to me? Huh? How she let him stay even after she found out? How about the fact that she wanted to keep my baby and raise it as my sister? My rapist's child, right there in front of me." The last of her words come out as a sob. I'm trying to control my anger as I walk over and sit next to her. I'm afraid to touch her so I don't.

"You gave her up though, didn't you?" Whisper asks softly. Steele moves back to his spot and Knox stands with his arms crossed over his chest leaning against the wall.

"I couldn't look at her with him there. I couldn't let them raise her. Look at me. What kind of person would that have made me? To let the same two people that ruined my life ruin hers." Tears stream down her cheeks as my heart crumbles inside of me. I judged her all wrong. What I knew, it was all wrong.

"God, Shane," Steele grumbles as he runs his hand over his face.

"I'm not helping her, Steele. I didn't agree to shit but she knew about the baby. I don't know how but she did, and she said that if I didn't want her dead that I had to help her. She said you had a sister that your dad killed." She sobs harder. I can't take it anymore. I grab her and pull her into my arms as she cries harder. My eyes move to Steele's as I try to comfort Shane. He doesn't look surprised by those words. He knew. Of course he knew; Steele knows a lot more about this family than any of us do. He had to. That's how he stayed alive when we were younger.

"Anyone else think it's time to kill that bitch?" Whisper asks, looking around the room. Steele chuckles and Knox snorts a laugh.

"You can't," Shane says in a panic. "She can't hurt her. She doesn't deserve that!" I keep my grip on Shane, as I look to the guys.

"She's right. We can't let her hurt an innocent child, not again."

"We need to dig boys. We need information on the adoption. Find out where that little girl is and get her protected first. If Carol was able to find her, it shouldn't be hard for the three of us," Knox says.

"Five." We all look at Whisper. "There are five of us." Steele nods his head and for the first time in a long time, I feel like this family is finally coming back together. Like we are who we were meant to be. I keep my hold on Shane as we discuss a few more things. She doesn't push me away and I'm grateful for that although I would understand if she did. I hurt her. I wrecked her for no other reason than being a prick.

Once everyone is done talking and a plan is formed, I stand and help Shane from the couch, leading her down the hall and up the stairs. She starts to go left but I pull her to the right. She doesn't fight me on this either. Opening the door to my room, I usher her in and follow behind her, closing the door behind us.

"I'm sorry, Callan. I know you must hate me, I hate myself."

"Do you know what I thought?" She shakes her head. "I thought you were with him. That's how it all looked. I thought you gave up your baby because you didn't want it, the way my mom gave us up. And I hated you for it, Shane. More than I could ever hate anyone. I wanted you to pay for something that you had no control over." Her eyes meet mine and I see the way she looks at me. I shake my head. "Don't. Don't try and make it okay for me. I was wrong, Shane. I had no idea what you went through and I made your life hell for it. I pushed you, toyed with you, and for what?" She steps closer, her hand resting on my chest.

"You couldn't have known everything, Cal. I never told anyone. It wasn't your fault."

"It was my fault."

"You said that I took something that should have been us. What did you mean?"

"That baby. She should have been ours, Shane. God, I have loved you since the moment I laid eyes on you. I would have given you the world if you wanted it." Tears fall down her cheeks as she looks up at me. I reach up and cup her good cheek before leaning in and kissing her. It's wrong. I shouldn't let myself do this. She should hate me.

"Hate me, Shane," I beg her. She shakes her head and kisses me back.

"I can't," she whispers against my lips. Everything I've fucked up in the past has come down to this.

"As much as I love you, I can't let you love me back, Shane."

20

SHANE

He tells me to hate him, not to love him. He tells me to forget everything but how can I when he keeps me so close? Every night since that night weeks ago I've been tucked into his bed with him wrapped around me. He hasn't made a move to touch me and God, I have tried. I want him. Maybe even more now that he knows everything, but he's keeping me at arm's length.

"He loves you," Steele says as I bring the bottle of whiskey to my lips.

"He hates me. He won't even kiss me," I say as I take another pull. Steele laughs as I look out at the sun as it sets.

"Day drinking doesn't suit you, Shane."

"Now ask me if I care." Why won't he just go away? I don't need him here. I don't need a babysitter.

"No, you don't care. You don't give a shit because you're angry and you need an outlet. Drinking works sometimes but maybe you need more."

"I'm not Whisper."

"Never said you were. She lets out a lot of steam by dancing. You should try it."

"Or fucking but I can't seem to get that either," I inform him. He laughs and I can't help but smile with him.

"Fine. We could always play a little game I like to call pool house," he says, eyeing me.

"I've heard about that from Whisper and I don't think that's really my thing. Thanks for the offer though."

"Come on. I'll drive you over to the studio." Steele grabs the bottle of whiskey and tosses it through the air. I watch it land in the grass as I drag my ass off the chair. Following him around the house, I climb in the front seat and buckle up.

"It's been weeks. Where the hell is she?" I ask more to myself than to Steele. He puts the key in and starts the car up, turning the radio down when music blasts through the speakers.

"She's a calculating bitch. Don't worry about her, Shane. Callan has made sure everywhere you go there is extra security, and he's working overtime to find that little girl." Pain slices through my chest when he says that.

"I never wanted to give her up you know? She was perfect in my eyes even though how she came to be wasn't." Steele doesn't say anything else as he pulls out into the road. We ride like this for a few minutes when he finally talks.

"We can find her. Get her back."

"No. I couldn't take her from her family, Steele. That would make me no better than your mom," I admit.

"You know we can make it happen. Just say the words." I turn my head and look out the window instead of acknowledging that. I know they could and that scares me a little.

We pull up to the dance studio and I climb out feeling a little buzzed from the amount of whiskey I drank. Following Steele inside, he holds the door as I walk past him. Knox looks up from the desk with some new girl they are training. I sigh. I'm losing my place here, too. Defeat is a bitch to swallow.

"Don't even think that shit," Steele growls near my ear.

"What shit?"

"That you're being replaced. I know what you're thinking and that's not it. Callan has other plans for you." I look up at Knox because this is news to me. Callan hasn't said two words to me since the night I spilled my past to them. It's a little strange to lay in his bed every single night but not have him speak a single word to me.

"What?"

"Just go down and meet Whisper in the last room." Steele walks off and I drag myself down the hall. When I step inside the last room, I stop in my tracks. Whisper is in a tutu surrounded by little girls dressed much the same but they aren't dancing to ballet music. The sight in front of me makes me laugh out loud. Whisper spins and catches my attention, waving me over.

"What is this?"

"This is our new Sunday class. 'Hip Hop Divas.'" I laugh again and it feels so good.

"In tutu's?" She nods and wiggles her eyebrows before turning to the girls.

"This is Shane. She is going to be your new teacher! Are you excited?" New teacher? I can't even dance that well.

"What?"

"This is your class. They're all four and five."

"I don't get it. Don't they need like a real dance teacher? Like one that knows how to dance?"

"I've seen you dance." That voice sends a chill down my spine. I turn to see Callan walking toward me, sweat dripping from his body. He's been in classes most of the day, so it's expected. He walks closer, grabbing my hand in his and pulling me toward the door. Whisper laughs before she starts talking to the girls again. Callan leads me across the hall and into one of the other rooms, closing the door and locking it. My heart beats a little faster now.

I watch as he walks over to the phone docks and sets his phone in it before turning the volume up. Montell Jordan's *Get it On Tonight* remix starts blasting through the room. Callan moves to stand in front of me across the room as I watch him. I watch his shoulders roll, sweat still coating his flesh, begging to be touched. His hips begin to pop and I can't stop watching him. He moves so perfectly. Coming toward me, he crocks his finger at me, telling me to come toward him.

"I can't, Callan." He smirks, rolling his hips as he gets closer.

"I've seen you, babe. Come on. Let's see what you got." This is a switch. He isn't pushing me away. So I go with it. I start to move, just a little when he grabs my hip in his hand, jerking me closer. Closing my eyes, I let the beat fill me just like Whisper told me to do. Then I let it take over me. Each move feels right. Each roll of my hips, each touch of his warm flesh against mine is perfection. He spins me out away from his body before pulling me back into his chest. His eyes are burning with a fire that I wish I could touch. His hips jerk, pop forward and then roll as he holds my hip in one hand. The heat between us is stifling but I don't want it any other way. Grabbing the back of my neck, he spins me around as I duck under his arm before he yanks me closer—my back to his front. His lips come down on neck, slowly licking his way up until he meets my ear. Then he sucks the lobe into his mouth and I moan. The music is still blasting, the beat on fire but he's slowed us way down. His movements are slower, more calculated than they were and his lips never leave my skin. They keep moving, kissing, sucking until my legs shake.

"Callan."

"Shh, just feel it," he whispers in my ear as he moves us toward the wall. My face presses against the glass mirror as he sucks harder. Then he's pulling back slightly, pulling me off the glass and grabbing my chin so that I'm forced to look into his eyes in the reflection. I've never seen anything as fucking hot as this. Callan keeps moving his body but I'm still, stuck in a haze that he's created around us. His hands move over my body, wrapping around my stomach as he moves back in. Slowly his hips grind into my ass, his cock hard and ready. My cheeks flush, heat coiling inside of me.

"Turn around and watch me," he says, pulling back. I spin around and watch as he hits the floor rolling his hips. I've never wanted to be a floor until this very moment. Cal looks up at me under his dark lashes, hooded and lust filled. My mouth slowly parts as he jumps back up. He spins, grabbing at the button on his jeans. He kicks his shoes off, kicking them off to the side as he messes with the front of his jeans. Then they're down, his boxers with them. He nods at my clothes, raising an eyebrow when I don't move. Slowly I pull my shirt off and move to my shorts next. His eyes widen, his nostrils flaring as he holds his cock in his hand. He never stops moving either and the way his muscles cord and release with each movement has me wanting to jump the man.

"Come here, Shane." I move toward him, wrapping my arms around his neck. He rolls his hips and his cock presses into me. I moan, his lips coming to my chin. He sucks my chin into his mouth until I nearly lose my balance. His hands wrap around me, lifting me by the ass as he quickly stalks toward the other side of the room. Slamming me against the wall, his mouth devours mine. The slowness is gone, replaced by a feral version of

Callan. My panties are pushed to the side right before he thrusts into me. I gasp at the full feeling he gives me.

"Watch us. Watch me in the mirror," he growls before his thrusts pick up. Each slap of our bodies together, the way our sweat mixes and becomes one, that feeling is everything. He's everything.

I can't tear my eyes away from the mirror. I can't stop watching the savage way he's fucking me right now. His toned ass, the muscles in his back. I can see every little movement and God help me, I love it. I cry out his name as he pumps into me harder, deeper. Heat spirals out of control inside of me and I can't hold on any longer. I come hard, my teeth sinking into his shoulder. Callan growls and unleashes inside of me. Both of us are panting for air but he doesn't make a move to pull out of me.

"Did I hurt your face?" he asks softly, his lips brushing my neck.

"No."

"Good."

"What is this, Callan?"

"I don't know, Shane. I don't know."

21

CALLAN

"I don't care what you have to do. I said find her!" I roar into the phone.

"Still nothing?" Steele asks leaning against the door frame with his arms crossed over his chest.

"No. They can't find her. How the fuck is she in our goddamn town and no one can find her?" Anger claws at my throat. This is bullshit. It's all bullshit. Carol Alder has managed to go missing in the matter of a few days. We had people on her, watching her. Apparently they aren't as good as our dear old dad wanted us to believe or they are half-assing the job because he's no longer here. Either way that's earning them a death sentence.

"She's not far."

"Why did you never tell us what you knew? Or thought you knew?" Steele blows out a breath and moves into the room, sitting in the chair in front of the desk. It feels odd to be sitting in my dad's old office like this.

"I didn't have anything concrete. I didn't want to bother you guys with something I didn't have hard facts on. You and Knox were doing well in school and that's just the way it should have been," he simply states.

"And what about you? You think you didn't deserve more than what he handed you? He almost killed you, Steele." Steele cracks that dark grin of his and I shake my head.

"But did I die?"

"Fuck off." He laughs. Asshole.

"I'm here, Cal. I'm not going anywhere. Dad thought he could break me because I got too close. He should have covered his tracks a little better and maybe I wouldn't have found out so much. That was all on him. I just didn't think you and Knox needed to be dragged into it." I nod my head and run my hand through my hair before looking back at him.

"What's going on with Intensity?" With that question, his face hardens.

"Cleaning up. The structural damage was only on the south end so we can rebuild that. It won't take much."

"I can't believe that bitch actually tried to blow us up," I say through a dark chuckle.

"Me either. And she had the balls to come here before that?" he huffs shaking his head.

"We need to find her. You get anything on the little girl?" Somewhere deep down I want her found. I want Shane to have that peace of mind, to know that she's safe and out of harm's way but that hasn't been the case yet.

"Just that she was adopted out of Canton. I've got people on it. They'll find her." I nod when he talks again. "What's the plan when we do find her?" I jerk my gaze to his and sigh.

"Nothing. Just make sure she's protected until we handle this shit with Carol."

"And Matt?" he asks.

"That's an easy one. I planned on handling those two this weekend."

"That right? Were you going to fill us in on your vigilante shit?" he growls. This brotherhood of ours has worked so well in the past because we do things together. We never stray far from our pack and that's how we keep each other safe.

"I wasn't. I thought about it, but I wanted to handle this myself. Matt made this shit personal, Steele."

"I know that but that means nothing in the long run, and you know it. We're Alder's. We stick together. Always have, Callan. You can't change that now," he adds with a stern tone.

"Fine. I want Shane there though."

"Nope. Not a chance in hell." Steele shoves out of the chair and heads for the door, but I follow right behind him. He isn't fucking this up for me.

"She's going," I state.

"No, she's not."

"What are we talking about?" Knox asks as he comes down the steps looking between us.

"He wants to handle Matt," Steele says.

"And?"

"And I'm taking Shane."

"No, you're not," Knox states. Steele chuckles.

"This isn't your choice. It's mine! My plan, my way, my say." They both turn to look at me, eyes narrowed.

"Why? Give me one good reason why she needs to be there and then I'll decide," Knox says, challenging me.

"I've pushed her. I've messed with her head over something that wasn't even her fault, man. I said things, did things… I need her to see that I'm done. I'm done fighting this thing between us. She's mine and I want her to know that I protect what's mine."

Steele blows out a long breath, but Knox just stands there nodding.

"Fine. She goes," Knox says, brushing past us on his way to the kitchen. Steele turns to look at me, really look at me.

"You sure? You can't go around claiming her as yours and regret it later, Cal. It's not how we work." I nod.

"I've thought this over. I've fought myself, Steele. My heart never changes even though that bastard is darker than it's ever been. I still love her and there is nothing I can do to change that."

"Would you want to?" Her voice has me closing my eyes. I tip my head back and take a breath before turning to look at her.

"No," I say firmly.

"I don't know what to say here. I saw how you hurt but I also saw how you grew, Cal," he says with a shrug. "Who the hell am I to tell you what to do? You're a grown ass man." Steele slaps a hand across my chest before walking past me and giving Shane a smile. I turn and walk toward her, pulling her into my arms.

"I've fucked up a lot over the years but you were never a fuck up, Shane. You were what I wanted but my dad wouldn't let me have you. I didn't want you hurt, I just need you to know that." She smiles and presses her lips to mine, nothing else needing to be said. Her tongue sneaks into my mouth and I groan. When I pull back, I run my finger down the angry red mark down her face. The stitches are still in place but it's healing.

"It's ugly."

"It's beautiful," I whisper.

"It's ugly, Callan. Don't lie." I smirk at her little attitude.

"It's beautiful, Shane, and do you know why?" She shakes her head. "Because you lived. She could have really hurt you that day."

"What are you going to do to her?" I know why she's asking.

She's worried about her little girl and that kills me. I don't want to touch Carol until I know that kid is safe, but that's proving to be harder than I thought it would be.

"She isn't going to live for what she's done," I tell her. "Neither is Matt." Her mouth drops open as she looks up at me.

"What?"

"Did you think I'd let him live for hurting you? For taking something from you that you can never get back? No, baby. Not a chance in hell will he keep breathing."

"You can't do that." She steps out of my hold and I'm confused. I cock my head to the side and study her for a long minute before I ask, "Why not?"

"You can't have that on your conscience, Callan." I laugh darkly, the mood turning darker and darker.

"Do you think I haven't killed before?" I ask, cocking my head to the side. Her eyes flash to mine and in this moment, I know she's torn. Reality versus what she believes. Me versus who she thought I was. I step toward her, my hand coming to rest on her cheek, my thumb stroking her soft skin.

"Please don't," she whispers.

"You have to know, Shane. I'm not the good guy. Not when I grew up an Alder. We don't have that luxury. We were made into what we are today and there is nothing that can change that. The question now is; can you handle that part of my life?" When she doesn't answer me, anger surges inside of me.

"This is a lot, Callan."

"I know it is but you're not going anywhere."

22

SHANE

Sweat drips down the back of my neck as I pick up busted bricks and toss them into the bin. We've been at Intensity for hours cleaning up. The guys could have hired someone to come out and do this but they didn't want to. This club means something to them and they wanted to handle it themselves. It's admirable yet tiring all at the same time.

"Your ass is looking good in those little shorts," Knox says. I turn to look at who he's talking to when I see it's me. I flip him off and he chuckles before going back to cleaning.

"While we're all here, I just want to say thank you. Intensity has been something special to me for years and this just broke my heart," Leddy says, catching everyone's attention. It isn't just us that are here. The town has pulled together to help out and that's an amazing feeling. "This club, it's been my lifeline and I know many others that it's saved too." Her eyes fall on Whisper as she smiles back.

"We got this. This place means something to all of us. It's our outlet," Steele says. Everyone cheers before getting back to work. I see Callan across the room helping Steele load some of the bigger stuff. His shirts off, his muscles flexing. It's a damn sight to see.

"You're staring," Whisper says.

"So what? Look at them!" I state, waving my hand up and down to make my point. Whisper laughs and leans into me, wrapping her arm around my waist.

"He's happier now with you here."

"He said some things to me that threw me off a little."

"Like what?" I turn to look at her and shrug.

"Doesn't matter. I don't think I could leave him even if I wanted to."

"You can't." Glancing over my shoulder, I see those words came from Knox.

"I'm not a prisoner," I remind him.

"Maybe not but you still can't leave. He won't let you." I roll my eyes and go back to work when I hear Callan's voice thundering through the large space. Whisper and I share a look before looking to him. His phone is to his ear, his face a mask. It's hard as stone. I've never seen him like this before. I can practically feel the fury swirling around the room, kicking up dust like a tornado. Then he turns and looks at me. Something passes over his features and a dark smile curls his lips. He hangs up the phone, slips it into his pocket and says something to Steele but never takes his eyes off me.

"Oh, that is probably not a good look," Whisper says. "Which makes it even sexier. Damn."

Steele and Callan move through the room, coming toward us. Steele stops to tell Leddy something before he nods to Knox. Callan is in front of me in a few short strides, grabbing my hand and dragging me from the building. As soon as we step outside, I take a deep breath, glad to get some air in my lungs that doesn't have concrete particles attached to it.

"We have to move now."

"What? What do you mean?"

"Matt is plotting something. He and your mom are at the house now. We need to finish this shit with them," he says looking me in the eye. I shake my head slowly unsure of what to say.

"I don't know…"

"I want you there. I want you to see that he will never hurt you again, Shane. I need you to see that I love you so much that I will do anything for you." My mouth hangs open; words stick in my throat. Callan just grins at me.

"Do I have to help?" The words barely come out as a squeak. I'm not sure I have the stomach to actually hurt someone.

"No. I just want you to know he's gone," Callan clarifies, wrapping his large hand around the back of my neck and squeezing. "I'll understand if you don't want to, Shane. I just—" Before he can finish, I answer.

"I'll go." Another smile tugs across his face, this one lighter than the last. He pulls me closer, crashing his mouth against mine in a heated kiss that has me panting for more. When he pulls back the others are outside and ready to go.

"Two cars. I don't want anyone to see us pull up. We park a block over in front of Mason's house. When we leave, you go somewhere public, where there are people," Steele says as he looks between all of us.

"Why?" I ask. His eyes move to mine.

"We need to be seen. Even briefly. The cops are in our pockets, but we are playing with fire. Literally." I open my mouth to respond when Callan laughs.

"Gas stoves. They cause such a problem." The way he says

it, so casually as if the words meant nothing to him. I never saw this side of Callan. The deadly side. The side that is more and more like Steele every single day. It unnerves me to a point.

"That they are. You ready?" Knox asks Callan. He nods his head, rests his hand on my back and ushers me into the car. We all climb in, me, Callan and Knox in one, Steele and Whisper in the other. My heart starts racing as we drive toward my house. The home that ripped me apart. The home that *they* live in. I never felt like that place was home. It was a house. A place to live and sleep but that was it.

It takes minutes before we pull up to Mason's. I know him as one of the Alder's friends. That's about all I know about him. Callan leaps out like a man on a mission and I suppose he is. He grabs my hand when we climb out and walks to the trunk, popping it open. There he grabs a duffle bag and shrugs it over his shoulder.

"You had this ready?" I ask glancing up at him.

"I'm always ready."

"You got everything?" Steele calls out. Callan turns toward him and nods, slamming the trunk closed.

"Is there anything in that house you want?" Callan asks as we walk between the houses, right through their yards. Not that anyone would say a word to the Alder's.

"A few things in my room, if that's okay?" Callan stops walking just to turn and face me. His fingers come to my cheek and run over the healing cut like he always tends to do.

"Anything you want is okay, Shane. Anything." I don't stop to ask the meaning behind that because I don't know that I really want the answer. Instead, I turn and take a deep cleansing breath and follow the others toward the house. When we get closer, Steele raises his fingers pointing two around front, one around back. I know those directions are for the guys so when Callan grabs my hand and drags me around front, I know I'm with him.

"You have a key?"

"They never lock it," I tell him. He chuckles and shakes his head before looking at the door. I take a step, ready to go in when he pulls me back shaking his head. He stares at the knob, seconds ticking past before he finally nods his head. I turn the handle and walk in with him and Knox right behind me.

"What the hell are you doing back here?" Matt's angry tone is directed at me; I know it is. I almost cower when I remember the two men backing me.

"What? You didn't miss me?" I snarl. He stands from the couch and starts toward me when Callan and Knox step up next to me. His eyes widen before he starts to turn around only to find Steele and Whisper.

"What the fuck is this?" he asks, turning back to me. Callan leans down and whispers in my ear, telling me to go and get what I want to keep. I shake my head.

"Not yet." He chuckles and stands up straight looking at my drunken mother half-awake on the couch.

"This is… well it's a little payback," Callan says stepping closer to Matt.

"You're going to jail this time!" Matt roars but Callan is fast. He drops the bag and swings, knocking Matt to the floor before Whisper leaves the room. She comes back with two kitchen chairs, setting them in the middle of the room.

"Shane?" my mom says through her drunken haze.

"Shane what the hell did you do now? Being a little whore again I see," she laughs. I can't move. I'm stuck in place wondering what the hell I'm doing here. Whisper moves though. She grabs the front of my mom's shirt and rips her off the couch before punching her much the same as Callan did Matt. Steele and Knox move to grab them as Whisper comes to me.

"Come on. Let's get your stuff," she says, grabbing my wrist and leading me to the steps. I follow her up, a hollow feeling inside of me. I step into my old room and bile rises in my throat. I hate it here. I hate everything about it. Moving to the closet, I grab my bag and the box off the shelf before moving to sit on the bed. I can hear the guys laughing downstairs but when I pull the lid off the box, Whisper gasps.

"Is that her?" she asks softly.

"Yeah. I wasn't supposed to take pictures, but they left her with me for a few minutes. I snuck a few. And the hospital gave me this," I say, passing the little hat she wore to Whisper. She takes it in her hands and smiles.

"It's so small. I can't imagine a tiny human in there," she says. The reminder hurts. It's not like I was ready to have a child at sixteen years old. I wasn't but she was a part of me. She was a piece of me that I will never get back.

"I know. She was only six pounds. They said it was because I was so young." I share what the doctor told me.

"She's beautiful, Shane."

"She is." Taking a deep breath, I grab the hat and the photos and stuff them into my bag before standing from the bed. I swipe the tear off my cheek and keep my head held high. "I probably shouldn't keep these."

"Yes, you should. There's nothing wrong with remembering her," Whisper says, grabbing my hand in hers. She squeezes tightly before we both leave the room and head down the steps. When we walk back in the living room, I see them both tied to the chairs with gags in their mouths and Knox pinning Callan to the wall.

23

CALLAN

What he said to me made my skin crawl. My stomach lurched and I thought I was going to kill him with my bare hands. The thought has crossed my mind more than once in the last few minutes. Knox keeps both hands on my chest as I heave in breaths. That's when I see her.

"What's going on?" Shane asks, looking at me and Knox.

"A minor issue," Steele replies, keeping his eyes on Matt. The tension in the room is thick as her mom wriggles in her chair. She's trying to get free as if we would allow that.

"Which is?" Whisper asks this time.

"Which is none of your business. Go turn the stove and oven on," Steele orders her. I wait for her to protest but she doesn't. She turns and walks into the kitchen.

"This is it, Shane. Anything you want to say to them?" Steele asks, resting his hand on my shoulder. I slap Knox's hands away from me and walk toward them, then I grab her hand and jerk her body into mine. My lips hover near hers and I can feel the heat of her skin even through her clothes.

"There's no going back. No second chance," I say softly, her tongue slowly running across her bottom lip. My insides tremble and not from what's about to happen here. I lean in and kiss her gently before pulling back and turning toward them. My eyes bounce from his to her moms and back when she finally speaks.

"You two made my life hell. I thought I could get away from it all, from you but I couldn't. Even in my nightmares you were there. I can't wait to see you both rest in hell." With that, she steps back into my arms. I wrap them around her, holding her tight as I breathe in the scent of her hair.

"Go wait out back. Away from the house," I tell her before pressing my lips to the top of her head. She nods and turns to walk out with Whisper. Me? I step closer to Matt and smirk as I lean down into his space.

"You stole from her. You took a piece of her that she can never get back and you threw it all away. For that, you will rot in hell," I tell him before pulling my lighter free. His eyes widen as he thrashes in his chair. I look to my brothers and they both nod before we turn and walk out the front door.

"Last chance to change your mind," Knox says. I shake my head, light the paper and toss it into the house before we turn and take off. We run around to the back as the fire slowly courses through the house. I hear the boom from the gas and duck as we run farther away. That's when I see her.

"What the fuck?" I roar as I rush toward Shane. She's pulling herself off the ground when I get to her, pulling her to her feet. She's unsteady as I hold onto her.

"You shouldn't have done that!" Carol screams as she looks at the house in front of her. What does she care? I swallow hard and look at the other guys with her, none of them familiar to me but they all look as deadly as I feel right now.

"You stupid bitch!" Steele growls.

"You three will pay for this. For all of this!"

"You aren't making any sense, Carol," Knox states stepping closer to her. His arms are corded tightly, ready for a fight as I keep Shane on her feet. The little girl, Bella stands in front of Carol with tears falling down her cheeks. Her wide eyes are haunted as she looks between us. Carol presses the gun harder against Bella's temple as my stomach drops.

"You don't deserve any of this! Your father built those businesses not you! If anyone should have them, it's me. The wealth, the fame, all of it is mine," she yells. Steele chuckles darkly before stepping toward her too.

"Are you kidding me? That son of a bitch tried to kill me. He tried to kill my brothers and you think you deserve everything?"

"We've fought. We've done all the dirty deeds that have kept this family afloat since the day we were born. We were the pawns that no one wanted and the strength that everyone needed," I say through a clenched jaw. Every fiber in my being is begging to choke her, to take her life the way she is trying to take ours. How dare she after all these years?

"You're right. You were a pawn to him but not to me! You were my kids, my sweet little boys that he turned into monsters." My eyes move from Carol's to Bella's and back. I don't know how it happened or what sense it makes but I see it now. It's all clear as day.

"How did you get her?" I ask Carol, nodding at Bella. She drags her focus back to me and shakes her head.

"She was a useful tool. When I heard about the baby, I knew my way back in." It must hit Shane at this very moment. She gasps, a sob that sticks in her throat.

"You're making a huge mistake."

"The only mistake I made was letting your father have you three. You've turned into such evil," she sneers.

"Says the woman holding a gun to a child's head," Knox says casually. So casually that I almost question his sanity right now.

"Well, now you've messed up. You ruined my plans and now I will ruin her," she says, eyeing Shane. I let her go, watching as she falls to the ground before I step around her.

"You know us, Carol. You know what we're capable of and you are testing the patience of a man that has very little at the moment." My words ring through the air as the sirens come closer. I have no doubt Blake will be on his way as well and that may just work in my favor. As long as I can keep Carol focused on me and not the gun in her hand, we might have a chance.

"I know what you can do. But do you know what I am capable of?" she sneers, thrusting the gun harder into Bella's temple. The soft cries that escape her break me in half. Before I can think about it, I'm moving. I don't hear anything aside from the rapid beating of my heart in my ears. I knock the gun from Carol's hand tackling her to the ground. Slamming my fist into her face, her head snaps to the side. The guys are moving around me, fighting the men that Carol brought with her. Me? I grab Bella and rush away from Carol and straight to Shane.

"Take her," I roar.

"No, I can't." she says, shaking her head rapidly. With my free hand, I grab her chin and force her to look at me.

"You can. She needs you now, Shane. Take her." It takes seconds for her to pull Bella from my arms and into hers. She holds her tightly against her chest as she cries. Whisper steps up out of seemingly nowhere and wraps them both in her arms. The sight in front of me is the most devastating and beautiful thing I've ever seen.

24

SHANE

My hands are trembling as I sit in the emergency room waiting room. Blake brought me, Whisper, and Bella here. He basically knew most of the details of what happened, but Whisper filled him in on the rest. He didn't question us like I thought he would. Instead, he brought us here and said that Bella needed to be looked over. Now we wait and I can't stop shaking.

"She's okay, Shane."

"She's a little girl that had a gun to her head. Who knows what else Carol did to her? What if she's hurt in other ways?" Whisper tenses at my words knowing exactly what I mean. It's not like she didn't live that life once before too.

"She is as strong as her mom. She's got this," she adds, making me smile a little. It doesn't take long for the doctor to come back out with Bella walking right next to him. She has a sticker on her shirt and an unsure smile on her face.

"She looks good. You can take her home," he says. I stand

from my seat and move toward her slowly before kneeling in front of her.

"My name is Shane."

"I know," she says softly.

"You do?" I ask, cocking my head to study her little face. She nods her head, her hair tumbling over her shoulder. She's so perfect. So beautiful.

"Yes. Carol told me. You're my mommy," she says softly and my heart leaps.

"She… she told you that?" Bella nods and I can't help the tears that fall down my cheeks. It almost shocks me when Bella reaches up and wipes them with her little fingers.

"Miss Carol said we should only cry if we're sad."

"Well, I'm not sad. I'm happy and it's okay to cry if you're happy too."

"It is?" she asks curiously.

"Yeah, it is. Are you ready to leave here?" She nods as I stand and offer my hand to her. She reaches up without hesitation and grabs it in hers. I've never felt this kind of love, this kind of happiness in my life. I know it could be taken away at any moment and then I'll be left to the sadness of losing her again, but for now, I can't let go. I need this. I need her.

We walk outside when I see the guys leaning against the SUV. Knox elbows Callan who's looking at the ground by his feet. He slowly raises his head and we lock eyes from across the parking lot. Slowly, I walk toward him with Bella holding tightly to my hand. Whisper moves past us, heading straight for Steele. When Callan stops in front of me, he looks at me for a long second before grabbing the back of my neck and pulling my mouth to his. His kiss is quick and passionate.

"You're okay?"

"I'm fine. You?" His forehead rests on mine and I sigh.

"Perfect." He pulls away and looks down at Bella before kneeling in front of her, then he holds his hand out to her.

"I'm Callan. You remember me?" he asks. Bella slowly reaches out and places her small hand in his as she nods.

"Are you my daddy?" Another sob rips from my chest as Callan smiles brightly at her. He moves his gaze to mine for a second before looking back to Bella.

"Yeah. I sure am. You ready to go home?"

"Callan don't do that. Don't say things like that when you don't know what's going on! How can you do that?" I snap, pissed that he would give her such false hope. He doesn't know what's going to happen. The state could take her away. They could put her back into the foster system.

"So, Bella? What do you say? Want to go home and see where you will be living?" She nods her head like she's a little excited and he stands and tugs her along. I can't move. He can't just say those things. I can't have her little heartbroken the way mine was all those years ago. I watch as he introduces her to the guys and Whisper before he looks over his shoulder at me. His smile falls before he turns and walks back.

"What?" he asks watching me.

"How dare you? How dare you make her comfortable only to have her ripped away?" Anger overtakes me and I lunge at him. My hits connect but they don't faze him. After a few more, he wraps his arms around me, pinning my own against my body before lowering us to the ground.

"You need to calm down, Shane. All this fighting you're doing is making me hard," he hisses against my ear. That bastard. How dare he say that right now?

"False hope. That's what you gave her, you bastard!" Tears slide down my cheeks and I can't stop them. It hurts. It all hurts.

"It isn't false hope. You think I'm stupid, Shane? They are going to see that she belongs to you!"

"What?"

"You think I told Blake to bring you here for nothing? They are running the blood tests. I have the lawyer already on it." His words choke me. He's doing all that for me? For her? As I calm, he loosens his grip enough for me to turn around and face him.

"You are doing that for me?" He shakes his head.

"I'm doing it for us. Me, you, Bella. She needs a family and what a better one than us."

"You're so young, Cal. You don't need this on your shoulders. I can do this alone. I know I can. I'm stronger now than I ever was before. All because of you," I ramble when his hand comes up and grips my face roughly.

"Maybe you forgot the part when I said I wasn't letting you go. I want you, Shane, and she is yours. Ours. She is ours." Tears slowly leak down my cheeks as Callan leans in and kisses them away. Callan stands and pulls me with him. He wipes my eyes and we turn to walk toward the car. I see Steele on the ground, kneeling in front of Bella. Her face is lit up, a smile pulling across her face as we walk closer.

"What are you doing?" Callan asks him.

"Talking to my niece. I'm getting in a good word, so I'll be the favorite uncle." Seeing Steele even remotely interested in being an uncle is such a surprise. Even Whisper is standing there in shock.

"It won't happen. I'll always be the better uncle, ain't that right, Bella?" Knox asks. She looks over and nods her head having no idea what it is they are really talking about.

"How about we go home before she starts picking best uncles?" Callan says and my heart leaps.

25

CALLAN

A daughter. I always thought I'd have kids with Shane because I loved her so much. Even when we were younger, I knew there was something more in her that I wanted. It didn't matter how old we were, I knew. Now that we have Bella, I couldn't imagine my life without her. I watch her as I lean against the wall of the studio with my arms crossed over my chest. A smile on my face that could be replaced.

"She's too damn cute. A lot like her mom," Knox says leaning up next to me.

"Yeah, she is." Bella twirls with the other girls, smiling and even laughing when she falls on her ass. Her laughter is infectious. Shane grabs her hands and pulls her up before leaning down and kissing the top of her head. It's the perfect sight to see. She's happy, she smiles all the time.

"Did you talk to the lawyer?" Knox asks.

"Yeah. He will have all the paperwork ready as soon as Shane says yes."

"You think she won't?" he asks. I laugh. I know she will but that doesn't mean anything.

"Want to find out?" I ask, raising an eyebrow. Knox chuckles as the class ends and the girls run out the door. Bella runs into Knox's arms, hanging off his neck as she tells him about her fall. I move toward Shane, grabbing her by the wrist and pulling her into me, kissing her until she can't breathe.

"Marry me."

"Excuse me?" she says pulling back.

"You heard me. We're getting married."

"No, we're not. What the hell is wrong with you, Callan?"

"Nothing. Nothing is wrong except this. Everything in my life is perfect except for your last name. We're getting married. If you want a big fucking wedding later on, you can have it but for now we're doing it the informal way," I tell her. I'm not asking her. I'm telling her. I'm sick of not having what I want in life and now I'm taking it.

"This is crazy. You can't tell me what to do, Callan. We aren't ready for marriage." Her hands land on her hips in that sexy way she does and my heart nearly bursts from my chest.

"Why aren't we ready? I fuck you every night in a bed we share. What more do you want?"

"I don't know!" She throws her hands in the air while I laugh.

"Well I know. I want you. I want Bella. I don't care how old we are. I don't care what other bullshit excuses you have. I'm tired of losing everything I love; do you understand?" Her eyes fill with tears as she shakes her head. I grab her face in my hands, pulling her mouth to mine. After a punishing kiss, I pull away and just breathe her in.

"Are you sure? Taking on a child is a lot, Callan."

"I told you before that I wanted her to be mine. If things were different, she might have been, just not when you were sixteen.

She's everything to me, Shane. Just like you are. I want this. I promise you that I will show you every single day of my life that this is all I want. My family has been fucked since the day I was born. Don't you see that? I don't want that for you or her. I want us to be happy and together."

"Really?"

"Yes, really. Pay attention, Shane. You and Bella are all I want. There is nothing I want more," I tell her. She nods her head and I crash my lips against hers once more. The taste of her salty tears on my tongue makes my heart speed up.

"Did you win?" I hear Steele before pulling back and looking at him.

"Damn right I did."

"Wait? What? Win what?" Shane asks, looking around at my brothers confused.

"He said he wasn't giving you a choice. The asshole was going all alpha on you," Whisper laughs.

"Are you kidding me? You think you can tell me what to do?" Shane turns to look at me. I can see the slight anger but I also see that she likes it when I tell her what to do.

"Yeah, I do, Mrs. Alder. And once you sign the damn papers at the house, that little girl is going to be mine too." She gasps. "Don't look so surprised. The adoption papers go along with the marriage certificate, Shane. I wasn't joking about any of this." She reaches up and swipes the tears from her cheeks when Bella rushes in between us. I lean down and pick my daughter up, holding her in one arm and pulling Shane in with the other.

"What am I going to do with you, Callan?" She whispers.

"Just… stay with me."

The end.

AFTERWORD

Did you enjoy Stay with Me? Consider leaving a review and if you think you can handle more of the Alder brothers, get Knox's story here: http://bit.ly/Cryforme

Connect with Erin and find more of her hot romance books!

Connect with Erin! She loves her stalkers.

Newsletter:http://bit.ly/ErinTrejoNewsletter

BookBub:

https://www.bookbub.com/authors/erin-trejo

Facebook:

https://www.facebook.com/authorerintrejo/

Facebook Readers Group –Fire and Ice https://www.facebook.com/groups/1177887305577544/

Amazon:

https://www.amazon.com/Erin-Trejo/e/B00U0RXH80/

Twitter:

https://twitter.com/trejo_erin

IG:

https://www.instagram.com/authorerintrejo/